A rifle shot rang out, drilling the side of the cart

Pushing the corpse away from him, Bolan rolled out into the glare of the searchlight and rose to a crouch, spraying a stream of gunfire toward the enemy. He cut down two gunners, then quickly directed his fire toward the old water tower.

The searchlight shattered, plunging the field into sudden darkness. The Executioner leaned sharply to the right, grabbed the railing and swung to the ground as more enemy fire chopped at the cart, piercing the wood and nailing the corpse.

Rather than waste precious moments trying to reload the Ingram, the warrior hurriedly unclipped a frag grenade and pulled the pin, hurling the lethal bomb as far as he could.

The grenade detonated less than five yards from the base of the water tower. The concussive force undermined the supports, cracking them to the point that the tower crumbled under its own weight.

As he paused to catch his breath, Bolan triggered his mike and murmured a quick message to Grimaldi. "I'm in fix here, Jack. Time for backup."

Without the headset, there was no way to know if Grimaldi had gotten the message. As Bolan glanced up, he found himself staring into the bore of a 12-gauge shotgun....

MACK BOLAN.

The Executioner

DON PENDLETON'S
THE EXECUTIONER®
FEATURING MACK BOLAN®

DOUBLE ACTION

A GOLD EAGLE BOOK FROM
WORLDWIDE.

TORONTO • NEW YORK • LONDON
AMSTERDAM • PARIS • SYDNEY • HAMBURG
STOCKHOLM • ATHENS • TOKYO • MILAN
MADRID • WARSAW • BUDAPEST • AUCKLAND

First edition November 1992

ISBN 0-373-61167-6

Special thanks and acknowledgment to
Ron Renauld for his contribution to this work.

DOUBLE ACTION

To shrewdly conquer with fewest losses, start not with a headlong assault. Rather, slip behind your foe's lines and cripple his resources. Then you won't have to bring him to his knees. He'll already be there.

> —Sir Charles Heath
> from *One If By Land:
> a Memoir of War*

Kill a man who's armed, and you can always claim the fight was fair. But prey on the defenseless, and you've lost your moral ground.

> —Mack Bolan

THE
MACK BOLAN®
LEGEND

Nothing less than a war could have fashioned the destiny of the man called Mack Bolan. Bolan earned the Executioner title in the jungle hell of Vietnam.

But this soldier also wore another name—Sergeant Mercy. He was so tagged because of the compassion he showed to wounded comrades-in-arms and Vietnamese civilians.

Mack Bolan's second tour of duty ended prematurely when he was given emergency leave to return home and bury his family, victims of the Mob. Then he declared a one-man war against the Mafia.

He confronted the Families head-on from coast to coast, and soon a hope of victory began to appear. But Bolan had broken society's every rule. That same society started gunning for this elusive warrior—to no avail.

So Bolan was offered amnesty to work within the system against terrorism. This time, as an employee of Uncle Sam, Bolan became Colonel John Phoenix. With a command center at Stony Man Farm in Virginia, he and his new allies—Able Team and Phoenix Force—waged relentless war on a new adversary: the KGB.

But when his one true love, April Rose, died at the hands of the Soviet terror machine, Bolan severed all ties with Establishment authority.

Now, after a lengthy lone-wolf struggle and much soul-searching, the Executioner has agreed to enter an "arm's-length" alliance with his government once more, reserving the right to pursue personal missions in his Everlasting War.

1

Mack Bolan stood at the edge of a weathered pier at Lanschel Landing, a state park along California's coast, staring at the ocean through high-powered binoculars. He wasn't alone. Tourists crowded the pier in hopes of catching a glimpse of the magnificent gray whales that regularly passed along that stretch of the Pacific as part of their winter migration to the warmer waters of the south. Some of those without binoculars were trying to line up shots through the viewfinders of their cameras, and still others were feeding quarters into a row of weathered, coin-operated telescopes mounted at the westernmost railing.

When a small pod was spotted several hundred yards out to sea, the pier came alive with cries of excitement. Bolan pretended to be as interested as the others so as to not draw attention to himself. He hadn't gone there to watch for whales. He turned and focused on an inlet cove. To the casual onlooker, the Executioner could have been mistaken for an ardent naturalist admiring the overhead flight of gulls and broad-winged pelicans, or scouting for otters frolicking the frothy surf. In fact, the warrior's gaze was directed at the steep-pitched bluffs overlooking the cove, and instead of wildlife he was more interested in a man in an olive-colored windbreaker idly pacing the planked walkway that ran along the cliff's edge.

The man was Stasha Darvin, Iranian-born owner of a successful imported-rug franchise bearing his name, with stores in several California cities. By all accounts Darvin ran a legitimate business. But in addition to rugs, the man used his trade connections to import another less-benign foreign commodity—international terrorists looking to gain access to American soil. Several U.S. intelligence agencies had been tracking the man's movements in recent months on the suspicion that he was about to broker a major smuggling operation. The eight men he was "importing" were a crack team of Mertardan renegades, linked to recent bombings that had claimed nine lives at U.S. military outposts in the Persian Gulf. The theory was that the outlaw Blue Coalition of Mertarda, a small Middle Eastern country situated beyond range of any of the oil fields that had provided such international clout to its neighbors, was banding with other terrorist elements from Iran, Syria and the PLO in hopes of using rampant terrorism as a means to broker the same political concessions granted the OPEC cartel.

When enough intel had been gathered in recent weeks to change U.S. strategy from mere surveillance to shutting down Darvin's operation and bringing the Mertardan terrorists to justice, the White House had put through a call to Hal Brognola at the Justice Department. As coordinator of the nation's most highly prized teams of clandestine warriors, it was Brognola who'd tabbed Mack Bolan for this assignment. For the better part of a week, Bolan had been tracking Darvin, waiting for him to tip his hand. Now, if the Executioner's contact back at Stony Man Farm had correctly cracked the code of a transatlantic cable sent to Darvin's San Luis Obispo store two days ago, the Iranian was finally making face-to-face contact with an intermediary representing the Mertardans. It was Bolan's job to observe the rendezvous, then tell Darvin's cohort in hopes of being led to the terrorists, or at least learning the whereabouts of the U.S. target they planned to strike.

A chill in the late-day breeze rolling in from the ocean allowed Bolan to wear the hood of his jacket without drawing undue notice. The hood concealed a lightweight headset linked to a belt-clipped radio that kept the Executioner in contact with José Markrey, the FBI field agent who'd been tracking Darvin's movements for five weeks prior to Bolan's arrival on the scene. Markrey was posted in a panel truck in the nearby lot, monitoring each vehicle that pulled into the park. Once Bolan relayed a description of Darvin's contact, the agent would hopefully be able to match it with the right car and plant a homing device that would help in any subsequent surveillance.

But, as was common in the espionage game, players often had a way of failing to comply with an opponent's expectations.

"Got us a pedestrian," Markrey reported. "From the hotel across the street, I think. Man about five-ten, one-sixty, wearing navy blue sweats and a pea cap. Just might be our guy. Over."

Rather than use his condenser microphone, Bolan reached to his belt and tapped a signal button on the concealed radio to confirm that he'd received the message. He lowered his binoculars and glanced in the direction of the parking lot, which was crowded with several tour buses as well as the usual assortment of vacation transport. Markrey's nondescript truck was parked under a gnarly pine near the park's entrance on Scenic Way Drive, an access road linking the park with Pacific Coast Highway. In the background Bolan could make out another stand of pines, as well as the wood-shingle rooftops of the Seaward Breeze Inn.

The new arrival had just finished crossing the street from the inn. Bolan raised his binoculars and focused on the man as he paused briefly near the pagoda that served as the park's information center. He was dusky skinned and bearded, and his face had a languidly deceptive look of boredom as he lighted a cigarette and eyed a map of hiking trails. Bolan didn't recognize him, but he shared Markrey's suspicions that it was indeed Darvin's contact. It seemed an even surer bet when the man set out on a footpath that led toward the Iranian's position.

Since the sighting of the whales, nearly everyone in the park was converging on the pier, making it nearly impossible for Bolan to maintain his surveillance. He lowered his binoculars and discreetly wove through the crowd until he was back on the mainland, less than a hundred yards from the cove. There was no one else nearby, which allowed him an opportunity to touch base with Markrey on his two-way.

"Looks like you were right," Bolan said as he watched the stranger clear the last steps leading to the clifftop walkway. "Did you get a good look at him?"

"Affirmative," Markrey replied. "He looks familiar. I think the beard's a fake."

"Did you get a bug on Darvin's car?"

"Negative. Too much traffic to risk it. We'll have to make do with the homing signal."

"I'm going to try to get a little closer," Bolan said. "Over and out."

By now the man in the sweats had caught up with Darvin, and they were speaking together near the wooden railing at the cliff's edge. They had the area to themselves, and it was obvious that the rendezvous had been arranged in such a way to ensure the fewest chances for eavesdropping, which made it equally obvious that what the men were discussing was of paramount importance. It was unfortunate they'd been unable to plant a bug on Darvin. Bolan figured the sooner they could get the lowdown on the terrorists, the sooner they could be dealt with, and unlike Markrey, the Executioner had no patience for the drawn-out, largely passive tactics of spying. Bolan had earned the nicknames Striker and the Executioner because he was a man of action. If he were calling the shots, he'd have collared Darvin weeks ago and wrung the information out of him, one way or another.

For now, though, he was going to have to content himself with staying close enough to the enemy to fulfill his official mission. Of course, if he happened to get too close and the enemy was to force his hand, well, he'd have no choice but to handle things his way.

There were two ways he could get closer to the bluffs. He could circle up toward the parking lot and retrace the route taken by the man in the sweats. He'd have clear access to the upper walkway but would have to risk having the men get a good look at him as they walked past him after the rendezvous. He opted for the second course, which took him straight to the cove and up a series of steps to an overlook halfway up the side of the cliff. No one else was on the landing except for a young couple. They couldn't hear Bolan's approach over the pounding of the surf, and the woman gasped when the Executioner's six-two, two-hundred-pound frame suddenly came into view and she found herself staring into his hardened blue eyes. Bolan offered a nonchalant smile and traded hellos as he walked past, stopping at a spot where the walkway abruptly dead-ended. There were posted signs advising that the area beyond the railing was unsafe for hiking.

Bolan was now less than thirty yards from the cliff-tops. He could see the other two men on the upper walkway, engrossed in an increasingly animated conversation. Darvin looked to be the more upset of the two, and he gesticulated wildly with one hand as he spoke to the man in the sweats, who stood calmly shaking his head. Between the crashing of the surf and the relentless screeching of gulls, it was impossible for Bolan to make out anything that was being said, however.

Suddenly, and without warning, the man in the sweats sprang into motion, exhibiting an overwhelming burst of strength as he lunged forward, jerked the Iranian off his feet and heaved him over the upper railing. Darvin flailed his arms and let out a scream, matching that of the young woman standing behind Bolan.

"Oh, my God!"

The drop was precipitous, but Darvin still slammed twice into rock formations before landing in a sprawl on a small sandy beach at the base of the cliff. He lay still a moment until the tidewaters rolled past, slightly jostling his inert body and diluting the blood that flowed from a deep gash on his forehead.

The young couple was still reeling from shock when Bolan leaped into action. Keeping an eye on the man in the sweats, he bounded over the lower railing and began scrambling up the steep incline. The rocks were damp and slick, providing little secure footing, but there was ample brush growing out through the cracks.

Bolan's experience helped him reflexively grab for those most likely to support his weight. He covered ground quickly, hoping to reach the clifftop before being spotted.

No such luck.

The man in the sweats, glancing over the railing to make sure the fall had killed Darvin, saw the warrior negotiating the steep rise. His bland features remained expressionless as he pulled up his sweatshirt to reveal a Browning FN semiautomatic tucked inside the waistband of his pants. He whipped out the gun and braced his forearms on the railing to steady his arm as he drew down on Bolan.

Clutching a thick length of exposed tree root with both hands to keep from falling, Bolan was in little position to take cover. He froze in place, locking his gaze with the gunman above him. Time seemed to stand still as the warrior noted a barrage of detail—from the dark, almost lifeless eyes of the stranger to the gentle curve of his index finger around the Browning's trigger. Provided the weapon had a full magazine, there were thirteen bullets lined up and ready to charge out. Trapped in the gun's sights, Bolan felt that at least one of the slugs had his name on it.

2

The Executioner lunged to one side and pressed himself against the cliff. His knee collided with a jagged knob of stone, sending white-hot flames racing up and down his leg. He winced but fought off the pain. There were more immediate threats to be concerned with. A burst of 9 mm slugs chipped at the rocks a few inches from his face, and he felt a shard of shrapnel nick his left cheek. Shifting his weight to secure a better foothold, Bolan risked freeing his right hand and quickly unzipped his jacket. As he yanked his Beretta from its shoulder leather, another two shots hammered the rock around him.

The Executioner wasn't in a position to hope for much accuracy, but he leaned out and fired anyway. His 3-round burst came close enough to the mark to drive his assailant back from the railing.

Bolan's earplug had dislodged during the commotion and dangled in the fold of his hood. He could barely make out Markrey's urgent voice coming from the distant panel truck.

"What happened? What's going on? Over."

"Darvin just got iced by his contact," Bolan reported. "He might be headed your way. I'm going after him."

The Executioner didn't bother signing off. Keeping the Beretta in one hand, he scaled the last few yards to the upper walkway. As he swung himself over the railing, a nearby trash can clanged from the impact of a stream of bullets. Bolan dived to the planks as a second barrage of gunfire raked the cross beams to his right. He traced the trajectory of the shots and spotted a black Chrysler Imperial parked just off the shoulder of Scenic Way Drive a few hundred feet south of the park's entrance. The back door was open, and a gunman with an Uzi stood beside it, covering the man in the blue sweats as he sprinted to the car. Bolan had to hug the planks as parabellums pummeled the woodwork, seeking him out.

Pinned down or not, Bolan wasn't about to let Darvin's killer get away. He continued to lay low, crawling on his stomach until he reached a break in the railing, beyond which the land was flat and undeveloped, mottled with ragged clumps of scrub brush and bits of litter. There was a concrete picnic table twenty feet out into the clearing, and after taking a deep breath, Bolan broke from cover and zigzagged toward it. The Uzi strafed the ground around him, dogging his steps and then gouging away at the concrete once he reached the table.

By now the man in the sweats had reached the Imperial and dived into the back seat. His ally spent the last few rounds of his Uzi, then clambered into the car as it began to lurch forward, raising a cloud of dust on its way back to the main road.

Bolan rolled out from behind the picnic table and stood. He planted his feet and raised the Beretta, drawing the retreating Chrysler in his sights. He waited for an oncoming car to pass clear of his target, then squeezed off two successive 3-round bursts, the first directed at the car's back tires and the latter at the rear windshield. He missed the tires but managed to shatter the back glass. Almost immediately the Chrysler swerved sharply to one side and skidded to a stop.

The Executioner broke into a run, wincing at the pain in his knee as he tried to close the distance between himself and the car. He could see activity in the front seat and figured he must have hit the driver. He could also see the man in the blue sweats point his Browning out the shattered back windshield. Bolan tumbled to his left as the semiautomatic rattled away, stitching the earth around him.

As he sought cover, Bolan saw a familiar vehicle roll into view. José Markrey had taken up the chase, and the warrior instantly sensed that the FBI agent intended to ram his panel truck into the Chrysler in hopes of putting the vehicle out of commission before a new driver could get behind the wheel. In doing so, however, Markrey was leaving himself an open target for the gunmen in the back seat.

Bolan rushed back out into the open, hoping to draw fire away from Markrey, but it was a useless ploy.

The man with the Uzi had reloaded and both he and Darvin's killer fired at the approaching truck in unison.

The truck's windshield exploded, and a crimson spray filled the cab as glass and gunfire ravaged Markrey's head and upper torso. Dead or not, the agent's foot remained jammed against the accelerator, and the truck sped up as it veered across the median, clipping the front end of the stalled Chrysler. The collision was strong enough to send the truck into a tailspin toward the nearby cliffs. Clumps of weeds slowed it a little, but momentum carried the truck into one of the concrete picnic tables with enough force to flip it sideways and send it crashing through the walkway railing.

Back on the main road, the Chrysler's tires screeched wildly as a new driver floored the car's accelerator. Despite damage from the gunshots and collision, the car was still roadworthy. Black clouds of exhaust spewed out the tail pipes as it sped off toward the highway. Bolan briefly gave chase on foot, then resigned himself to the futility of it. He stopped on the shoulder, taking note of the vehicle's license number, though he knew full well that a check would probably reveal that the plates, if not the car itself, had been stolen.

Lowering his gun, Bolan caught his breath and was about to turn to check on Markrey when a loud, amplified voice boomed through the windy air.

"You! Drop the gun or you're dead!"

Bolan glanced over his shoulder and saw a Parks and Recreation four-wheel drive headed toward him. There were two rangers in the front seat, one behind the wheel, the other clutching a bullhorn in one hand and a double-barreled shotgun in the other.

"Right now!" the ranger with the gun commanded.

Bolan warily let his Beretta fall to the ground. As the vehicle pulled up beside him, he said, "Look, I'm a federal agent. My ID's in my right coat pocket."

The ranger with the shotgun climbed out of the vehicle and pulled a laminated card from Bolan's pocket, which identified him as Michael Belasko and claimed that he was a special agent with the Justice Department. It was a routine cover, and any call for verification would have cleared without any problem. The ranger didn't bother, though. He passed it to his partner, who gave it the once-over and passed it back, nodding his head.

"Okay, Mr. Belasko. My name's Fredericks and he's Horncastle," the ranger with the shotgun said as he handed the ID back. "You want to clue us in on what this is all about?"

Without going into unnecessary detail, Bolan quickly briefed the men and suggested they wire the Highway Patrol to try to intercept the Chrysler. "And get an ambulance," he concluded, gesturing toward the nearby cliffs, where the panel truck was barely visible, lying on its side amid the collapsed walkway.

"I'll handle it," Horncastle told his partner as he grabbed for a radio mike mounted under the dashboard.

Bolan and Fredericks hurriedly followed the errant tracks left by Markrey's truck.

"Lucky the whales were out today," the ranger observed dourly. "Usually a lot of families are up here...."

"We didn't come here planning on a shoot-out, if that's what you're getting at."

The ranger shrugged. "Yeah, I suppose you didn't."

Neither man spoke the rest of the way to the overturned truck. Ripped open where it had crashed into the picnic table, the truck tilted downward at a precarious angle, wedged between broken walkway slats that kept it from sliding the rest of the way over the precipice. From where they were standing, neither man could get a look at the front seat.

"Can't see the driver," Fredericks stated.

"I'm going to take a closer look," Bolan said, easing through the break in the railing.

"Better watch your step," the other man advised. "That whole walkway's been knocked off its supports."

Indeed, there was an ominous groaning under the warrior's feet as he stepped onto the planks. He jumped clear as the truck slid a few inches forward, splintering more wood under its weight. Landing beneath the walkway, Bolan grabbed for one of the foundation posts to keep himself from plummeting down the cliff.

"Holy shit," the ranger murmured up at the ledge, looking down at Bolan. "Are you all right?"

The Executioner didn't answer. He grimaced as he secured his footing and inched his way under the planks. The truck now lay directly above him, leaking gasoline and oil from its engine compartment. He could hear the dull groan of wood slowly giving way under the heavy weight of the truck. Bolan knew if he didn't move fast gravity was going to bring the vehicle crashing down on him.

Once he'd wriggled up past the posts, Bolan was finally able to catch a glimpse of the front seat. José Markrey lay on his side, still behind the wheel but pinned against the door by the collapsed roof. His face and chest were covered with blood and his right arm was twisted into an unnatural position at his side, but his eyes were open and he was breathing.

"Markrey!" Bolan called out. "Hang on, we're going to get you out of there!"

The agent wasn't able to turn to face Bolan. Staring out the shattered windshield, he feebly shook his head.

"G-g-go," he whispered hoarsely. Blood trickled through his lips.

"Not without you, pal."

Bolan knew the odds were against his being able to open the door and ease Markrey out, but he had to try. He reached out slowly for the door handle. Before he had a chance to get a secure grip, there was a sudden loud crack on the other side of the truck. A rail post snapped in two, and the truck teetered sharply away from Bolan's grasp. For a fleeting moment, Markrey was flung to one side so that his gaze fell on Bolan, filled with terror and resignation.

Then he was gone.

With a loud rumble, the truck broke through the walkway, dragging down shards of wood as it bounded off the hard rock and then became briefly airborne, spraying sand, blood and gas into the surrounding mist. Then the vehicle crashed loudly at the base of the cliff, landing in the white sand a few yards away from where the body of Stasha Darvin was still being toyed with by incoming waves. Gulls fled from the bedlam in a white flutter, echoing their shrieks off the rocky walls of the cove. Already several tourists, including the young couple, were making their way toward the rubble.

"What a goddamn mess," Fredericks muttered as he peered down from the edge of the cliff. He spotted Bolan still clinging to the treacherous incline and shook his head with disbelief. "Hell's bells, I thought for sure you were a goner, too."

Bolan climbed back up to level ground, then stood alongside the ranger and stared impassively down at the grisly tableau. It wasn't the first time he'd witnessed the carnage of a mission gone awry, and the odds were it wouldn't be the last. But it was something he knew he'd never get used to.

THREE MILES down the road from Lanschel Landing, the Chrysler pulled onto a dirt trail leading to the rolling fields of Whitson-Drew Vineyards. One of several small, lesser-known wineries operating along the central coast, Whitson-Drew was listed on paper as being jointly owned by seven limited American-born partners, but behind the paperwork the real owner was Prince Widdar Charn, playboy nephew of Saudi oil sheikh Leih Baibdi, acknowledged by many to be the most influential power broker in the OPEC cartel.

The vineyard was cordoned off by a long, rambling fence, and twenty yards in from the road was a barbed-wire gate. As the Chrysler pulled up, two field hands materialized, unlocking the gate and pulling it open so the battered vehicle could pass through. This was the back entrance to the winery, and the car drove along endless rows of staked grapevines before coming upon an old, ramshackle barn left as a reminder of the land's previous incarnation as a dairy farm. More workers were waiting near the opened main doors to the dilapidated structure. They waved the Chrysler through, then drew the doors closed, just as a Highway Patrol helicopter was first making its presence known as a growing speck against the horizon.

The vehicle rolled to a stop amid several haphazardly stacked bales of hay in the back corner of the barn. The car's rear doors swung open, and out stepped the man with the Uzi and the man in the blue sweats. Neither looked as if he'd sustained injury from

Bolan's Beretta. The driver, however, was bleeding from a shoulder wound, and as soon as he got out of the car he asked the others for help in dragging out the man who'd initially been behind the wheel. The man in the blue sweats set his Browning on the roof of the Chrysler and lent his comrade a hand. Together they reached across the front seat and pulled out a man whose skull had been pierced by a 9 mm shell.

"Poor Raiko," the man with the Uzi lamented as the dead man was carried to a nearby stall and laid out on a bed of straw.

"Our brother died for a good cause," the man in the blue sweats said. "His death will be avenged."

"I hope so." The man with the Uzi sounded skeptical.

"He was my brother, too, Atmon," the man in the blue sweats said.

"I know that, Ehki," Atmon said evenly. "And I also know what Charn will say. He'll say Raiko died for the greater good, and in achieving the greater good we will have our vengeance."

Ehki Daifreize nodded as he began to peel off the false beard he'd worn for his rendezvous with Stasha Darvin. "Yes, I'm sure that's what he will say."

"That isn't good enough!" Atmon clutched his Uzi and waved it emphatically. "The man who killed Raiko must die! *That* is the only acceptable revenge."

"I agree. And it shall be."

Atmon slowly lowered his gun, letting his rage subside. "Do you promise?"

"You have my word, Atmon." Ehki Daifreize turned from his brother and faced the man who'd taken the wheel after Raiko's death. "There's no exit wound in your shoulder. The bullet must still be inside you."

The wounded man nodded. He was perspiring, as much from the pain as anything else. "Yes. I can feel it."

"Atmon," Ehki told his brother, "see that Amin is tended to. Make sure no one spots you from the air."

The man nodded, then led Amin past the workers lingering near the doorway. Left alone in the stall, the man in the blue sweats dropped to a squat and stared down at his slain brother.

"They have something here in America called poetic justice, Raiko," Ehki whispered to the corpse. "It means one gets what one deserves." Ehki quickly frisked the dead man, taking out his wallet and emptying it of cash and identification. His face was etched not so much with grief as anger. "You were greedy, little brother. I heard the rumors about you wanting more power, about your trying to cut deals on your own behind my back. I was wondering how I was going to bring you back in line. Now a stranger has solved the dilemma for me. I'll have to find a way to thank him."

Ehki stood, smiling enigmatically. "*Then* I'll kill him...."

THE SUN HAD YET to touch down over the ocean, but the moon was out and the first stars of evening were already winking to life overhead. High tide was gradually claiming the entire beach area of the cove at Lanschel Landing, forcing the authorities to hurry about their business. The park had been closed down shortly after José Markrey's truck had crashed, but the area was still bustling as search teams scoured for any physical evidence Stasha Darvin might have brought along to his ill-fated rendezvous with the man in the blue sweats.

Bolan stood amid the commotion, reluctantly supervising the preliminary phases of the investigation. He hadn't bargained on such a task. He would have preferred that no local agencies be on the scene to get in his way, but they'd descended on the park minutes after the altercation in hopes of claiming their share of the action. Bolan had been left with little choice but to try to contend with the inevitable chaos resulting from interaction between law-enforcement agencies. On the positive side, Bolan's Justice Department credentials made him first in line for receiving any news of recent developments. Thus far, however, the news wasn't encouraging.

"No trace of the Chrysler," a Highway Patrol officer told Bolan "Our guess is they ditched it somewhere before the freeway and switched to another car."

"Makes sense," Bolan conceded as he watched paramedics pull the zipper up over the mangled corpse of Markrey, enclosing him in a full-length body bag similar to the one that Stasha Darvin had already been placed in. Both bodies were placed on a stretcher, which was then affixed to cables dangling from the underside of a Highway Patrol helicopter. Once the paramedics stepped back and signaled the pilot, the copter ascended, hoisting its grim cargo toward the ambulance parked where Markrey's panel truck had crashed through the clifftop walkway.

"We *did* trace the plates through DMV," the officer told Bolan. "Somebody swiped them off a Honda Accord in the parking lot at Hearst Castle day before yesterday."

"Figures."

"Yeah. We're still running a computer check for any reports on stolen Imperials, but no word yet."

"Probably won't be much help anyway."

"Never know. We might get lucky."

"That'd be a change," Bolan muttered.

The patrolman excused himself and began following the two paramedics up the winding pathway that would eventually lead them to the top of the bluffs. Bolan watched waves lap at the half-submerged remains of Markrey's crushed panel truck. Two FBI agents in scuba gear were salvaging as much from the vehicle as they could, transferring it to a pile on the rocks to Bolan's left. It would be a couple of days before the wreckage could be towed away. In the meantime it would lie there, drawing as much attention from park goers and curiosity seekers as any schools of migrating whales.

The media had been given a cover story that the incident was nothing more than a drug bust gone sour, but details were necessarily scarce.

Bolan just wished he was a lot less in the dark than the public. He felt a growing frustration with the way things were adding up. There were two men dead and not a hell of a lot to show for it. If anything, they'd lost ground. After all, with Darvin they'd at least had a handle on one of the middlemen. Now that he was dead, he couldn't lead them either to the terrorists or those attempting to smuggle them into the country.

"We're losing the light," one of the scuba men called out as he emerged from the shallow surf, carrying some of Markrey's drenched surveillance equipment. "We could bring in some kliegs and make a night of it, but we've got the truck picked pretty clean and I doubt if anything else is going to turn up."

"You're probably right," Bolan said. "Why don't we shut down and just post a couple men here for the night."

"Sounds good to me."

The agent set down the surveillance equipment and wandered over to confer with the others. Bolan took a flashlight and shone it on Markrey's things, hoping some telltale clue might present itself. It didn't seem likely. None of the wiretap equipment had been brought into use that day and there were no notepads, no microcassette recorders that might contain some useful information.

There was, however, a camera. It was damp to the touch, and the telephoto lens was cracked, but the case was still sealed. Bolan felt a prick of hope as he crouched to check the film guide, realizing that at some point Markrey had snapped off nine shots.

"Hey," he called out to the scuba diver, "was this camera submerged at all?"

The diver shook his head. "Markrey was wearing it around his neck, and the straps got tangled in the rearview mirror somewhere along the line."

"Then the odds are the film's intact."

"I guess so," the diver said with a shrug. "Have to check with a shutterbug to be sure."

"I'll do that," Bolan said. He could only hope, however, that what was inside would be able to grant him a few wishes.

3

The two surviving Daifreize brothers left the barracks that housed the live-in work force at Whitson-Drew Vineyards and walked side by side across the vast estate.

Once out of the blue sweats and false beard, Ehki Daifreize struck a handsome, imposing figure. Unlike his brothers Atmon and Raiko, who'd always been wary of embracing American fashion, Ehki had taken a fancy to Western wear. Clean-shaven, with his jet-black hair combed slickly back with a layer of styling gel, the Saudi wore python-skin boots, well-weathered jeans and a fringed leather jacket over his Pendleton shirt and bolo tie. Strolling casually past moonlit rows of grapes, he looked more like a seasoned cowpoke on his way to kick up his heels at a barnyard hoedown than a Saudi Arabian native who'd never been near a horse until he was in his mid-twenties.

In sharp contrast Atmon wore simple khaki slacks, work boots and a black turtleneck. Haggard and misty eyed with grief, he continued to lament the loss of their younger brother and swear vengeance against Raiko's killer. Ehki listened with quiet patience, offering token comfort but secretly wishing he could drop the pretense and get away from Atmon before he betrayed his lack of any real remorse over Raiko's death.

"I say we should track down Raiko's killer now!" Atmon said. "Tonight!"

"Don't be foolish, Atmon. We don't even know who it was, much less where he might be."

"We can find out!"

"Enough!" Ehki turned on his brother, grabbing him by the shoulders. He moved in close so their faces were only inches apart. "Listen to me! When the time is right, we'll see about revenge. But not tonight. It's not smart and we aren't going to do it. Do you understand?"

"Let me go!"

"I said, do you understand?"

Atmon jerked his brother's hands from his shoulders and lurched away. Sullen eyed, he glared at his brother but said nothing. Ehki matched Atmon's stare as well as his silence, and after several prolonged seconds, he turned his back on his brother and strode off. Atmon waited a moment, then warily followed a few steps behind.

It was the slowest time of the year at the winery. Most of the harvesting had taken place the previous month, and new plantings had been made in the deep-plowed soil of the northern fields the week before. That left only tending to casks and bottles of wine in the storehouse and the pruning of existing vines. Halfway to the mansion, Ehki stopped at a clearing where several workers were gathered around a bonfire of day-old cuttings. In the shifting glow of the flames it was difficult for him to guess the nationality of the workers. The majority of the vineyard's labor force consisted of Hispanics, some with papers and others without, but there was also a corps of transplanted Saudis handpicked by Prince Widdar Charn not only for their ability to pass as Mexicans, but also because of their steadfast allegiance to the winery's secret owner. These were the workers who had helped bring the Chrysler Imperial onto the property and secret it in the old barn earlier in the day. If by chance lawmen had managed to follow the Chrysler into the winery, the Saudis would have drawn weapons and willingly fought to the death to ensure that their benefactor's cover wasn't revealed.

One of the men broke away from the others and approached Ehki. He was tall and lean, with a lightning-shaped scar under his right eye. Ehki recognized him as one of the men who'd helped usher them to safety earlier.

"I have a message from the prince," the scar-faced man said.

"He's not here yet?"

The other man shook his head. "He'll be coming later, once he's sure we aren't under surveillance."

"And how will he know that?" Ehki asked as Atmon joined them, avoiding his brother's gaze in favor of glaring balefully into the crackling fire.

The man with the scar smiled faintly. "I have a friend. A radio dispatcher with the sheriff's department."

"I see."

Ehki tried not to betray his disappointment with the delay in meeting the prince. After what had happened at the park, he was wary that the authorities would set out a dragnet in hopes of snaring him and his cohorts. He was anxious to leave the area as soon as possible and get on with the mission. But he couldn't do that until after he met with Widdar Charn to report on his rendezvous with Darvin. He had no choice but to wait.

"He left word that you could wait for him at the mansion," the other man reported. "The cooks are preparing dinner."

"Very well." Ehki sighed and called over the other man's shoulder to his brother. "Atmon, let's get something to eat."

He thanked the scar-faced man and started off. Atmon silently followed. They hadn't gone more than a few yards before Ehki stopped and looked back. The man with the lightning scar was following them.

"May I have another word with you?" he asked.

Ehki let his impatience creep into his voice. "What is it?"

"Your car," the other man said. "The Chrysler. We put it in back of one of our delivery trucks. When it's safe we'll haul it from the vineyard and leave it someplace where it will throw the authorities off the scent."

"Good. That was the plan."

"Yes, but I want you to know I'm taking care of it personally." The scar-faced man shifted his gaze back and forth between the two brothers. "You have nothing to worry about."

Ehki stared hard at the other man. "Did I say I was worried?"

"No. No, of course not. I just wanted to assure you."

"And what else?"

"I beg your pardon?"

"You have something else on your mind," Ehki prompted. "Make it fast."

The other man exhaled and chose his words carefully. "I'm glad for the chance to serve the prince by working here. But this is all manual labor and the occasional errand. I'm meant for better things."

Ehki frowned. "Why are you telling me this?"

"When you meet with the prince perhaps you could put a word in for me," the other man told the brothers. "My name is Beroq. I'm good with guns and not afraid of danger."

"And you want a chance to prove it," Ehki Daifreize guessed.

"Yes! I haven't been told what your mission is, but perhaps you could use more help. You lost your brother, plus there was another man wounded. You'll need replacements, won't you?"

"Perhaps."

"Any of the others will vouch for me," Beroq said, indicating the other men standing around the fire. "All I ask for is a chance. I'm sick of grapes and wine."

"But not sick of whining, eh?" Ehki sneered.

Beroq was taken aback. "No," he protested. "I don't mean to complain. Only to suggest that I—"

"I'll consider what you've said," Ehki said, cutting the other man off. "For now, though, see that you tend to whatever job the prince has assigned you to."

"Of course," Beroq said. "And I promise you, give me a chance and you won't regret it."

"We shall see." Ehki glanced at his brother. "Come on."

Atmon quietly fell in stride beside Ehki and they walked off. Beroq watched them, then trudged back to the bonfire.

Ehki rolled his eyes as he withdrew a pack of cigarettes from his coat pocket. By the time he'd lighted one, he'd already forgotten Beroq's name. The last thing he was interested in was bringing a newcomer into his fold. He'd already been nearly undermined by his own flesh and blood; he wasn't about to start placing his faith in complete strangers.

Atmon felt differently, however. As they neared a grove of orange trees, he told his brother, "I'm not all that hungry. Why don't you go ahead without me?"

Ehki shrugged. "If that's what you want."

Atmon nodded. "I'll feel better after I get some sleep."

"I think so, too." Ehki placed a hand on his brother's shoulder. "I'm sorry I yelled at you. It's been a hard day. For all of us."

"I understand," Atmon said. "I'll see you in the morning."

"Yes, and I'll let you know how the meeting with Widdar Charn went."

Ehki flicked his cigarette into the dirt, then plucked an orange from one of the trees as he headed through the grove toward the mansion. Atmon stayed put a moment, then retraced his steps to the bonfire, seeking out Beroq and drawing the scar-faced man aside.

"Were you serious about wanting a chance to prove yourself?" Atmon asked.

"Absolutely."

"This friend of yours," Atmon said. "Can you get in touch with him tonight?"

"Her," Beroq corrected. "I plan to see her when she gets off work. I want to find out the best place to ditch your Chrysler."

"I want to come with you," Atmon said. "I want to see if your friend knows the man who killed my brother."

"Ah. And if she does?"

"If she does, then you'll have your chance to prove yourself," Atmon said. "You can help me track the man down and kill him like the dog he is."

"Tonight?" Beroq asked.

"Yes," Atmon told him firmly. "Tonight...."

"LEAVE IT TO JOSÉ," the bald man with thick bifocals said as he emerged from the darkroom holding a sheet of photographic proofs. "He was the best."

"Then he got something?" Bolan asked.

"You bet," the bald man replied, his voice filled with both pride and sadness at the loss of a good friend. "Have a look for yourself."

They were in San Luis Obispo, at the FBI's make-shift field office in an old downtown brownstone that was undergoing major renovations. The bald man, Mookie Sandhoff, was a Bureau lifer, once a crack field agent but now content to provide technical assistance from the sidelines. He'd been asleep at his trailer home on the other side of town when Bolan had called him from Cinnaton, but as soon as he'd heard about Markrey and the film that had been found in the slain agent's camera, Mookie had roused himself and hustled to prepare the darkroom for Bolan's arrival. The effort was worth it.

"This is even better than I was hoping for," Bolan admitted as he scanned the proofs. He was expecting shots of the man in the blue sweats, and there were seven of them, two taken with a regular lens while the rest were from the telephoto lens. In all but one of the shots, the man in the sweats was in clear focus.

"There's the best one of the bunch," Mookie said, pointing to a shot of the stranger pausing to light a

cigarette at the park pagoda. Markrey had clicked the
shot just as the man's lighter was at full flame, illuminating his features. As Markrey had suggested, it
did look as if the man's beard was fake. Even with his
pea cap pulled down low over his forehead, the man
wasn't able to fully conceal his features. The eyes,
brow, nose and cheekbones were all well-defined and
quite distinctive.

"We can blow that one up and airbrush away the
beard and have something to match up with mug
shots," Mookie suggested.

"Good idea. How about these?"

Bolan directed Mookie's attention to the last two
shots, which Markrey had apparently taken just before leaving the parking lot to meet his unexpected
demise. The shots were of the Chrysler, taken from the
passenger side, apparently as it had pulled onto the
shoulder near the park entrance at Lanschel Landing.
The front window was rolled down, and a man in the
front seat was peering through a pair of binoculars.
Bolan tried to picture in his mind the position of the
parked car in relation to the direction the binoculars
were pointed. He quickly realized that the man was
most likely observing the walkway, either during the
rendezvous between Stasha Darvin and the man in the
blue sweats or the latter man's attempt to gun Bolan
down as he was scaling the cliff to reach the walkway.

"Let me have a closer look at those," Mookie said,
unsnapping an old weathered velvet-bound case and
pulling out a magnifying glass. He held the glass over

the proof sheet, concentrating on the shots of the car. "I can't blow these up too much without losing detail, but you might be able to get a make on the guy with the binoculars. Maybe the driver, too, but I doubt it."

"Give it your best shot, would you?" Bolan asked. "Then we'll try to circulate some photos to all the hospitals and morgues in a hundred-mile radius. Maybe I nailed somebody when I shot out the back windshield."

"Well, it's sure worth a try," Mookie murmured over the ringing of an old rotary phone on the desk behind him. "Let me take this call, then I'll get right on it."

"Fine."

"Bureau," the bald man barked into the receiver. He listened to the caller a moment, then muttered, "Just a sec. Hey, Belasko, it's for you."

Bolan took the receiver as Mookie headed back into the darkroom. "Yeah?"

"That you, Striker?"

"Sure is," Bolan answered, recognizing the voice of Hal Brognola. Responding to the Executioner's request for someone to handle the vagaries of interagency bureaucracy, earlier that evening the big Fed had flown in to California from a conference he'd been attending in Dallas with Stony Man Farm's ace flyboy, Jack Grimaldi. They'd quickly joined up with FBI agents in San Luis Obispo who were conducting a search of Stasha Darvin's rug emporium as well as his home.

"How'd the photos turn out?" Brognola asked.

"Good," Bolan reported. "I think they're going to be a big help."

"Glad to hear it, because we're going to need all the help we can get."

"What'd you find out?"

"We're at Darvin's house," Brognola reported. "It's just a couple of blocks from where you are. Come by and I'll tell you in person."

"I'm on my way."

Bolan hung up the phone and knocked on the darkroom door, telling Mookie where he was headed. Letting himself out, the warrior headed down a flight of steps and out a main hallway leading to an atrium. The space was filled with various construction materials, and Bolan had to step around a tall stack of paving tiles to reach a second stairway leading down to the street. He took the steps two at a time until he reached the sidewalk, then headed for his rental car, parked just in front of the building.

Across the street a truck was parked in the half shadows between streetlights. Atmon Daifreize was sitting in the front passenger seat, filled with anticipation and rage at the sight of the man who'd killed his brother. He slowly closed his fingers around the door handle, preparing to swing it open. In his other hand was his Uzi submachine gun, safety catch off and ready to fire.

It was time for revenge.

4

As Bolan unlocked his car he heard the distinctive sound of another car door opening. It wasn't the loud, unguarded clack made by someone paying little heed to what he was doing, but a drawn-out metallic groan. The Executioner tensed and shifted his gaze just enough to detect a change in the reflection of light off the passenger window of the truck across the street. Instantly he knew someone was trying to slip out of the vehicle without tipping himself off.

Someone with less combat sense might have hesitated a few seconds to evaluate the situation and plot a course of action, but for a warrior a few seconds often spelled the difference between life and death. Bolan reacted instinctively and dropped to a crouch even before getting a look at the man across the street. Anticipating gunfire, he let his momentum carry him quickly to his right so that he could use the car as a shield.

Atmon Daifreize jumped down from the truck and leveled his Uzi, blasting out the rental's windows and pounding holes in its body. He couldn't tell whether he'd hit his target, so he retreated to the front of the truck and quickly reloaded as he cursed himself for having given his quarry a chance to reach cover.

Bolan came up from his crouch, Beretta in hand. He was about to squeeze off a 3-round burst at his opponent when yet another gun barked to life behind him, almost nailing him in the back. The Executioner dived forward, landing in the litter-strewn gutter just as the rear tire of the rental ruptured, pierced by a succession of slugs.

Ambush.

Beroq, who'd driven Atmon to San Luis Obispo after learning of the whereabouts of Raiko's killer through his dispatcher friend, was firing his .357 Magnum from behind the concrete centerpiece of a large, unfinished fountain situated in the middle of the office building's courtyard.

Bolan held his fire, not about to waste ammo until he had a clear target. With one tire blown out, there was barely enough clearance for him to crawl beneath his car, and as he inched his way under the chassis, a third assailant let loose with a blast from an old Belgian FN rifle. The rental's headlights exploded and the radiator was perforated.

Crawling on his belly, Bolan peered out from under his car. He caught a glimpse of the rifleman, who was firing from the doorway of an office building twenty yards away. Switching the Beretta to its single-shot mode, the warrior held his breath, drew a bead on the sniper and pulled the trigger.

The third man was one of Beroq's close friends from the winery. He was about to empty the rest of the FN's 20-round magazine at Bolan when a 9 mm bullet slammed into his chest, ripping through cloth, flesh and bone before lodging in his heart. The rifle clattered off its rounds as the man fell forward, but he was already dead and the shots danced wildly across the sidewalk, posing little threat.

That left Bolan still pinned between two known assailants, and he had no way of knowing if others lurked in the darkness. He stayed put a few moments longer, but when the Uzi took out two more tires, the Executioner had to move quickly to avoid being crushed underneath the settling car. There was no room to his right, so his only option was to roll into the street, placing himself directly in the subgunner's sights.

Instead of the staccato rattle of the Uzi, however, Bolan was surprised to hear the crash of broken glass, followed by the commanding thunder of a Government Model Colt automatic. He traced the sound to the second story of the nearest building and saw Mookie standing behind the broken window, driving the gunner to cover with the .45.

"Thanks, Mook," Bolan murmured under his breath.

A police siren began to howl in the distance, drawing closer by the second. Chased by slugs from the .357 Magnum, the Executioner sprang to his feet and rushed to the doorway where the fallen rifleman lay dead in a growing pool of blood.

Bolan holstered his Beretta, snatched up the FN and swung it toward the courtyard. When he spotted the man with the .357 moving amid the shadowy contours of the fountain sculpture, he pulled the trigger. Rapid-fire rounds from the FN riddled Beroq's midsection, doubling him over in pain. The Saudi lost his footing and toppled from the sculpture, landing facefirst in the fountain's dry basin.

Atmon, meanwhile, exchanged fire with Mookie, shattering more glass and splintering wood on the second-story window frame. Bolan took advantage of Daifreize's distraction, propping the butt of the Belgian FN against his shoulder and slowly swiveling the rifle to his right until he had the sights lined up with the side of the man's head.

"Drop your gun!" Bolan ordered in the vague hope he could take the man alive for questioning. But the gunner swung around, Uzi still clutched in firing position, leaving Bolan no choice but to pull the trigger.

Atmon jerked backward as the shot ripped away half his face. His Uzi fell to the street, and he landed next to it. Bolan's shot echoed a few seconds longer off the surrounding buildings, then the street fell silent except for the howl of approaching sirens.

"Nice shot," Mookie called down from the second floor.

Bolan lowered the rifle and looked up. "Thanks. You saved my bacon, too, you know."

Mookie grinned as he held his Colt .45 for Bolan to see. "Yeah, for somebody half-blind and half-bald I didn't do too bad."

"You did great," Bolan assured him. "I owe you one."

Mookie shook his head. "If any of those bastards down there are the ones that killed José, we're even."

The first of three black-and-whites squealed around the corner and braked to a stop near Bolan's rental car. The Executioner was in no mood to have to deal with the police, but under the circumstances he doubted that he'd have much choice. As officers piled out of the first car, guns drawn, he sighed and reached for his Belasko ID.

"No need for the hardware," he told the cops, gesturing at the crumpled body next to the winery truck. "Showdown's over."

Once the police had assessed the situation, a call went out for ambulances. Already the streets were beginning to teem with curiosity seekers drawn by the sound of sirens and gunfire. The police began to cordon off the area as Mookie came down to help Bolan answer questions.

Several minutes later, the Executioner spotted two familiar figures being let past the barricades. The older of the two, Hal Brognola, looked somewhat fatigued in his loose-collared shirt and slightly rumpled suit. Jack Grimaldi was more casually dressed and seemed ready for action. Bolan excused himself and left

Mookie to deal with the police as he joined his colleagues from Stony Man Farm.

"When you didn't show up and we heard all that racket, we figured you were up to no good," Grimaldi taunted his long-time cohort.

Bolan shook hands with both men, then quickly related what had happened, concluding, "I'm not positive, but I think at least one of these guys was in that Chrysler earlier today."

"That would make sense," Brognola said, glancing at the winery truck. "And unless I miss my guess, we'll probably find the car in the back of that truck, or at least evidence it was in there at some point."

"Let's find out," Bolan suggested.

The three men led several policemen with flashlights over to the truck. Grimaldi and one of the cops went to check the front seat while the others circled around back. The freight doors weren't locked, and once they were opened, a quick glance inside revealed a hydraulic ramp designed specifically for loading smaller vehicles. Bolan borrowed a flashlight and climbed up into the truck.

"Looks like you win a cigar, Hal," he said, directing the light's beam at the hardwood planks, where a small puddle of oil and muddy car tracks provided further proof that a car had been stored in the truck recently. "They must have ditched the Chrysler on the way into town."

Grimaldi rejoined the group as Bolan jumped back to the ground. "Truck's registered to some outfit called Upcold Enterprises, but there's a lot of paperwork in the glove compartment belonging to some winery up in Cinnaton. Whitson-Drew.''

"Hmm," Brognola mused. He drew Bolan and Grimaldi away from the others. "I remember half the wine in Stasha Darvin's cellar came from Whitson-Drew. Seems like more than just a coincidence.''

"I'll say," Bolan replied. "I remember driving past their place on the way here. It's just down the road from Lanschel Landing.''

"So they probably stashed the car there," Grimaldi said, "which explains why Highway Patrol didn't spot it anywhere.''

Bolan glanced away a moment, watching the police inspecting the bodies of the three men who'd tried to gun him down. "Well, obviously we're going to have to pay a visit to Whitson-Drew and find out how they fit into all this.'' He turned back to Brognola. "You said you found something at Darvin's place. It was more than just the wine, wasn't it?''

"Oh, yes. Quite a bit more, actually.''

"Jackpot," Grimaldi said.

"The terrorists?'' Bolan asked.

"No," Grimaldi confessed, "but we've got a pretty good idea where they'll be headed.''

Brognola reached inside his coat pocket, pulling out a plastic bag containing a folded sheet of paper. "Topo map," he said, handing the evidence to Bolan. "Alaska.''

"Alaska?" Bolan frowned as he opened the bag and unfolded the map. There was a clear plastic template taped to the map, and the only marking on it was a jagged line reaching from Prudhoe Bay on Alaska's oil-rich North Slope down to the shipping port of Valdez.

"The pipeline," Grimaldi stated.

"The terrorists they're trying to smuggle in are explosive experts," Brognola said. "Stands to reason they're looking to blow up the pipeline."

"Why?"

The big Fed stared at the map a moment, then looked back up at Bolan. "Let's hope we can get to them before we find out the hard way."

5

The evidence linking Whitson-Drew Winery with the terrorist smuggling operation was compelling but, at this point, circumstantial. Brognola knew the legal system would require something more substantial before official measures could be taken. He was in the process of having a warrant drawn up authorizing a thorough search of the vineyards, but it was going to take at least a few hours. Given the situation, the big Fed was wary of letting too much time pass.

And so it was that Mack Bolan found himself stalking the perimeter of the winery under a midnight moon. Wearing a lightweight Kevlar vest under his snug-fitting blacksuit, his face darkened to make him blend further into his nocturnal surroundings, Bolan considered this essentially a surveillance mission. But if worse came to worst, he'd forsaken his Beretta in favor of the mightier punch provided by a Desert Eagle .44, and clipped to his waist along with extra ammo cartridges was a string of six grenades, half of them flash-bangs and the others deadly frags. An ankle sheath held a ten-inch Pall survival knife and strapped to his thigh was an Ingram submachine gun. All the gear had been customized by Stony Man Farm's crack weaponsmith, John Kissinger, to shed excess size and weight as well as to increase performance efficiency and reliability. Consequently Bolan was able to move without feeling constricted or slowed down.

Grimaldi had dropped him off on Lefnich Drive, an offshoot of the main road that circled around the back acreage of the winery. A closely planted row of cypress pines ran just inside the barbed-wire fence, providing privacy for the vineyard—and an ideal screen to mask Bolan's entry to the property.

Unsheathing his knife, the warrior crouched beside one of the wooden posts supporting the barbed-wire fence. Implanted in the knife's hilt was an adjustable-intensity flashlight. Bolan shed a dim beam and scanned the post for remote sensors. Finding none, he put another of the knife's accessories to use, snipping at the barbed wire with a spring-loaded bolt cutter located just above the handle. In less than a minute he'd cleared an opening large enough to slip through.

"Mercy to Flyboy. I'm in," he whispered into the same button mike he'd used at Lanschel Landing. Tonight, however, he'd forsaken the headset, unwilling to compromise his hearing once he'd penetrated enemy territory. Grimaldi could pick up his transmissions and hopefully track Bolan's position, but there was no way for the pilot to return communication.

"Converting to homing signal," Bolan said. "Over."

He flicked the small switch on the underside of the microphone, then sheathed the knife. He advanced through the pines to a narrow stream that trickled along a broad stretch of relatively barren silt land, unsuited for growing vines but handy for draining the vineyards. Far off in the distance Bolan could see a dilapidated barn, an old water tower, the workers' barracks and the stately mansion. Smoke rose from a smoldering heap of cuttings, and the dying flames silhouetted several workers standing around the heap. The only other activity Bolan could see was that of someone posted on the mansion roof. A sentry, he presumed. And if there was a man posted up there, even more guards had to be prowling the grounds. To Bolan that alone lent credence to suspicions that this was more than a mere winery. It also meant he would have to be on his guard.

There was little in the way of cover along the stream or surrounding silt land. Rather than risk exposure, Bolan took the long way, backtracking into the pines and following them until they finally connected with the outermost rows of vines. This section of the vineyard hadn't been pruned yet, and the rows were dense enough to allow Bolan to get halfway to the barn without being seen.

An untended wooden cart had been left at the end of one of the rows. Bolan paused briefly beside it, then set out again, only to freeze when he heard a sound coming from inside the cart. He dropped to a squat, closing his fingers around the handle of his knife.

Boards creaked inside the cart and Bolan also heard a bottle roll to a stop against the wall less than three feet from his head.

A dazed worker, who'd apparently dozed off in the cart after downing a bottle of wine, stifled a yawn as he slowly sat up. The moment his gaze fell on Bolan, the man's jaw dropped with shock. He was about to shout when the warrior lunged forward, clamping his left hand over the man's mouth. At the same time he thrust the knife into the worker's chest at an upward angle, bypassing the sternum and skewering the heart. The worker slumped back, landing on a thin layer of straw. Rising on the cart's wheel spokes, Bolan leaned over his victim, twisting the knife as he continued to smother the man's dying cries.

The Executioner had tried to make the kill silent, but there was just enough noise to betray him. As Bolan pulled his knife from the dead man's chest, a bright shaft of light suddenly cut through the night air, falling on the cart. He dived to one side, pressing himself against the walls of the cart and dragging the dead man toward him.

The searchlight fell on the body and there were shouts from above. Bolan didn't dare raise his head to trace the source of the light, but in his mind's eye he recalled the layout of the vineyard and realized that the old water tower next to the barn must have been converted into a lookout post. The light had to be coming from there. Shouts were coming from the grounds, too, and the warrior suspected that guards were on their way to investigate the commotion.

With the cart enveloped in the harsh glare of the spotlight, Bolan knew that as soon as he showed himself he'd be a sitting duck for whatever firepower the men were wielding.

He was trapped.

PRINCE WIDDAR CHARN'S reputation as a spoiled hedonist wasn't without foundation. Orphaned as a child and subsequently raised at his uncle's lavish estate in Saudi Arabia, Charn was afforded the best life-style and most opportunities that petrodollars could buy. For the most part he took his wealth and privilege for granted, squandering small fortunes on a seemingly endless indulgence of whims and fancies. As a rampant consumer, it was inevitable that he'd end up living in the States, where he could have ready access to the marketplace. He traveled in high-society circles and often threw lavish parties for celebrities and other well-heeled members of the jet set, earning himself regular mention in *Vanity Fair, Interview,* and a number of other glitzy periodicals tracking the life-styles of the rich and famous. It was largely through his depictions in these magazines that the world in general came to view Charn as an essentially harmless social butterfly.

There was, however, another side to the prince, a side that was more barracuda than butterfly. Behind his frivolous facade lurked a keen, malicious mind,

and there was more to his carousing with the upper
crust than an unquenchable appetite for good times
and frivolity. A master of manipulation, Charn befriended people in order to put them off guard and
calculate their weaknesses, the better to exploit them
for his own benefit. Through guile and cunning, during the ten years he'd been in the States he'd managed
to amass a personal fortune that, while not rivaling
that of his uncle's, was substantial enough to place
him high on the list of the Fortune 500...provided he
was to go public with his true worth. That wasn't
likely, however, since Charn felt such a proclamation
would only weaken his bargaining position on the
world stage.

No, Charn preferred to wield his clout behind the
scenes and out of the public eye, just as he was doing
tonight at Whitson-Drew Winery.

Pacing the oak-paneled tasting room, Charn sam-
pled some two-year-old chardonnay as he patiently
listened to Ehki Daifreize's explanation of what had
happened during his rendezvous with Stasha Darvin at
Lanschel Landing.

"...and I knew there were going to be problems as
soon as he began talking about troubles with his business." Daifreize was seated at a long hardwood table
in the middle of the room, sipping mineral water
rather than wine. His feet were crossed and propped
up on the chair next to him, polished python boots
gleaming under the lights of a chandelier dripping with
crystal. When he'd first begun working for the prince

he'd been more deferential, but in time he'd come to realize that although Charn demanded blind and humble obedience from his immediate entourage of bodyguards and servants, he was more apt to admire bravado and arrogance in those assigned to carry out his business agenda.

"He wanted more money," Charn guessed.

Daifreize nodded. "Double."

Charn sighed, pausing to pick up a different glass of wine. He sniffed around its rim and made a face.

"This won't do at all." Charn shook his head at the only other person in the room, an elderly, stoop-backed man who served as the winery's cellar master. The steward's look of expectation turned to disappointment as he made a notation in the ledger opened before him on the table. Charn's disapproval meant six hundred cases of would-be premium Chablis were going to be downgraded and shuttled off to a subsidiary for marketing as a low-priced table wine.

The prince set down the wine and resumed his pacing. "Double?" he said to Daifreize. "He didn't really think he could get away with that, did he?"

"Apparently." Daifreize took out his cigarettes and tapped one loose from the pack. "He said he'd done some rough calculations of the increased profits you and your uncle would be making if the pipeline was knocked out of commission, and he figured that he was being underpaid."

"He was probably right," Charn said with a smile. "That will teach him to play with calculators."

Daifreize let out a spirited laugh, then lighted his cigarette and blew a quick series of smoke rings at the chandelier. The cellar master frowned and coughed as the rings widened and drifted his way. Charn told the old man he was through sampling for the night, and the steward gratefully left the room, closing the door behind him.

"Anyway," Daifreize went on, "I humored him and said that we could meet him halfway. He was suspicious. He wasn't sure if I was authorized to make such an offer without your approval."

"He was right again."

"Of course he was," Daifreize said, paying little heed to the implied threat in the prince's voice. "And I told him as much. I said that if you wouldn't come up with the extra money, I'd pay him out of my cut."

"How generous of you."

"That's what he thought, too." Daifreize chuckled, tapping ashes into the wineglass containing the ill-fated Chablis. "Once I told him that, I had him eating out of the palm of my hand."

"So he gave you all the information?"

Daifreize nodded. "Trusting fool. He spelled out all the details." The Saudi reached into the pocket of his Western shirt and withdrew a small plastic case that contained a microcassette tape. "Names, timetables, everything we need to know to bring in the Mertardans."

"And you're sure it was all legitimate? He could have been lying."

Daifreize shrugged. "I know that, but it all rang true. Of course, I'll have to verify a few things before we proceed, but at the time I had to go on a hunch. I guessed he was being straight."

"Let's hope you're right."

"I usually am."

"And after he gave you the information?"

Daifreize blew more smoke. "He wanted to be paid, of course. As we'd agreed on."

"But—"

"But," Daifreize said, "I said there'd been a delay in getting the cash together. I told him if he could wait a few days, I'd pay him both the installments we'd agreed on, then he'd get the bonus once we'd gotten the men into the country. He said that wasn't acceptable. It was like he snapped. He started swearing, threatening me, threatening to blow the whistle on the whole operation."

"So you killed him."

"That's right," Daifreize said. "I threw him over the railing. I wanted to make it look like it'd been an accident or that he'd jumped, but when I looked over the railing to make sure he was dead, I saw this man climbing up the side of the cliff. It was incredible! He was like this human fly, just coming right up after me."

"Any idea who he is?"

"Not really, but if Darvin was being tailed, my guess is FBI, maybe INS. I'll make some calls tomorrow to find out for sure."

"I'm sorry about your brother," Charn said.

"*C'est la vie.* You play this game, sometimes you lose."

Charn poured himself wine from one of the bottles that had passed his inspection earlier. "I remember you saying that Raiko was becoming too big for his britches. That he was looking for more power."

"It was becoming a problem. He was trying to get Atmon to side with him against me. That wouldn't have been acceptable."

"And now?" Charn asked. "Will Atmon remain loyal?"

"I think so. It might help matters if we could track down the man who shot Raiko and see that he's killed. Atmon is thirsty for vengeance."

"If it's convenient," Charn said. "Otherwise, Atmon will have to get his satisfaction from the success of the mission."

"Exactly."

The prince poured a second glass of wine and handed it to his subordinate, then raised his own glass for a toast. "To the mission."

Daifreize tapped his glass against Charn's. "To the mission."

Once they'd shared their toast, Daifreize began to spell out the details of Darvin's plan to smuggle the terrorists into the country. They were only a few minutes into their conversation, however, when there was a sudden urgent knocking on the door.

Charn glared at the door and shouted, "I left orders we weren't to be disturbed!"

The door opened and the cellar master meekly ventured in, his face white with terror at having to be the one to deliver bad news.

"Forgive me, Your Highness," he gasped, "but we have an intruder!"

IN THE PROCESS of reaching for his Ingram, Bolan inched just far enough out of the shadows that the guards in the water tower could see him. A rifle shot rang out, splintering the uppermost wall of the cart. Bolan knew he had to act, and quickly.

Pushing the dead man away from him, he rolled into the glare of the searchlight and rose to a crouch, spraying a stream of gunfire along the ground. He cut down two men rushing toward the cart, then quickly directed his fire up at the water tower. The searchlight shattered, plunging the field into sudden and, for Bolan, welcome darkness. He leaned sharply to his right, grabbed the railing and swung himself down to the ground as more enemy fire chopped at the cart, some of it piercing the wooden walls and nailing the dead man.

Bolan guessed there were at least half a dozen men on the ground firing at him and another two up in the water tower. He evened the odds a little when he strafed a row of vines on the far side of the cart, downing another two gunners. There was no time for self-congratulation, however, as return fire from the enemy pelted the dirt around him, forcing him to dive headlong for the faint cover afforded by a furrow of newly dug soil.

Rather than lose time trying to reload the Ingram, Bolan hurriedly unclipped a frag grenade and pulled the pin, then hurled the deadly egg as far and wide to the left as he could. As he waited for the inevitable explosion, he switched over to his Desert Eagle.

With a thunderous boom, the grenade detonated less than five yards from the base of the old water tower. There was enough concussive force to undermine the supports, cracking them to the point that the tower crumbled under its own weight. There were screams of terror as the two snipers posted on either side of the disabled searchlight were pitched over the railing. It was more than sixty feet to the ground, and both men were dead on impact.

The ground forces hadn't seen Bolan throw the grenade, and the explosion scattered them to cover, wary that they were contending with more than one intruder. Bolan sensed as much and took advantage of the lull to rise from the furrow and sprint around a row of vines to the old barn. He slipped in through a gap in the upright slats and crouched near the opening, the .44 clenched in his right hand.

As he paused to catch his breath, Bolan triggered his button mike and murmured a quick message to Grimaldi.

"I'm in a fix here, Jack. Time for backup."

Without the headset, there was no way to know whether Grimaldi had gotten the message. As he glanced up and found himself staring down the bore of a 12-gauge shotgun, Bolan's first thought was that it didn't matter if help was on the way.

6

The khaki-clad sentry stepped farther inside the stall, his shotgun leveled at the Executioner's face. True, he had the drop on Bolan, but only because he'd refrained from pulling back the hammer on his antiquated 12-gauge. The weapon wouldn't fire until he did so, and the split second it took was all the time Bolan needed.

He leaned away from the line of fire and torqued his body in such a way that his right foot whipped around with forceful accuracy. He kicked the shotgun's barrel just as the gun went off, and the blast flew wide, obliterating a section of the barn wall.

The warrior followed through with a quick succession of well-placed blows with his left foot and the callused heel of his right hand. The sentry reeled backward into the side of the stall, cracking half-rotten boards under his weight before landing in an old feed trough. Stunned by the impact, he flailed his legs and was about to let out a cry when Bolan pulled out his Desert Eagle and aimed it between the man's eyes.

"One word and you're dead!" the Executioner whispered in Spanish, not wanting to take the chance that the sentry couldn't understand English. While it was true that for Bolan the focus of his mission had shifted from surveillance to survival, he still wanted some answers, and here was a prisoner who could hopefully be made to talk.

The other man whispered hoarsely, begging for mercy. His Spanish was more fluent than Bolan's, but the Executioner sensed that the man wasn't speaking his native language. Given the nationality of Stasha Darvin and the men slain in the failed ambush back in San Luis Obispo, Bolan figured the man for Middle Eastern. He leaned forward, pressing the tip of the Desert Eagle against the man's forehead.

"Your boss," he said. "Who is he?"

The man trembled, swallowing hard as fear-induced adrenaline raced through his system. Both he and Bolan could hear other guards converging on the barn.

"Who's your boss?" Bolan repeated, nudging the gun barrel deeper into the creased folds of his prisoner's forehead. "Tell me!"

"Ch-Charn," the sentry whimpered. "The prince."

"Widdar Charn?" Bolan asked, recalling the name from a recent briefing at Stony Man Farm regarding the political makeup of the OPEC cartel. "Leih Baibdi's nephew?"

"Yes!"

"What's he have to do with the winery?"

"I don't know. I swear!"

"Where is he now?" Bolan demanded.

"The mansion. He came here tonight, to meet with—"

They were interrupted by the sound of someone charging into the barn. An overhead light suddenly flickered to life. Bolan sprang away from the trough as bullets ripped into the stall. The sentry took two rounds in the midsection and screamed in pain. The warrior whirled and fired at the shotgun-wielding guard who'd turned on the lights. Blasts to the chest and face killed the man even before his limp body crumpled to the ground.

Bolan next directed his fire at the naked light bulb dangling from an old cord in the middle of the barn. The bulb exploded, sending a faint shower of sparks to the ground. None of them managed to ignite the loose straw, but they gave Bolan an idea. As he rushed past the fallen sentry near the light switch, the Executioner unclipped a flash-bang grenade from his belt. Pausing near the doorway, he pulled the pin and hurled the grenade into the hayloft.

Charging out of the barn, he ducked gunfire from yet another sentry and dived for cover behind a large section of the fallen water tower. As the guard chased after him, there was a sudden explosion, and shrapnel hurtling from the barn knocked him down. Bolan finished him off with his Desert Eagle, then waited a few seconds to make sure that flames had taken hold inside the half-demolished barn. As soon as he saw thick clouds of dark smoke roiling through gaps in the collapsed roof, and telltale flickers in the loft, he sprang from cover, eyes on the distant mansion. He was in the middle of a hell zone, the lone target of more men than he could count, but the Executioner had his sights set on his destination, and he was determined that no one would stop him from reaching it.

"DAMN IT!" the prince shouted as he stared out at the fire and bedlam in the nearby vineyards. "How many of them can there be?"

Enough to cause them problems, Ehki Daifreize quickly realized.

They'd moved from the tasting room to the kitchen's large walk-in pantry. Next to a shelving unit holding dry goods was a small window that overlooked the grounds. The two men were crowded in front of it, Daifreize holding his Browning semi-automatic while Charn clutched the tape player containing Stasha Darvin's plan to smuggle the Mertardan bomb squad onto American soil. The window was closed, but they could still hear the exchange of gunfire. As they watched, yet another of Charn's hand-picked warriors fell victim to whomever had infiltrated the winery.

"And now they're coming by air!" Charn pointed to the northern sky, where winking lights betrayed several helicopters sweeping over the bordering stand of cypress pines.

"Well, let's not just wait around for them to get to us." Daifreize moved from the window and reached for the door to the kitchen. "Your car must be out back. Let's go—"

"Never mind the car!" the prince interrupted, blocking Daifreize's way. "Why do you think I led you here to the pantry?"

As Daifreize eyed the prince skeptically, Charn reached above the shelves, fingering a switch concealed behind a length of decorative molding. There was a dull clicking sound, then the entire shelving unit swung clear of the wall, revealing ladder rungs connected to the far side of a two-foot-wide cavity in the wall.

"This way," Charn said, gesturing for Daifreize to enter the opening. "Get in and start climbing down!"

Daifreize warily complied, squeezing into the tight space and lowering himself, rung by rung. At first there was enough light pouring in from the pantry to light his way, but when Charn followed him into the enclosure and closed the secret entrance behind him, they were plunged into darkness.

"It's about twenty feet down," Charn called to Daifreize, "then we'll come to a tunnel."

Sure enough, after several more rungs down the ladder, Daifreize felt his left foot land on solid ground. He stepped clear of the ladder and waited for the prince to join him. Once Charn was on level ground as well, he groped along the wall, seeking out a light switch. He flicked it on, and intermittently spaced lights revealed a tall, narrow tunnel extending away from the mansion and under the winery grounds.

"It was first built as a bomb shelter in the 1950s," the prince explained as they started down the passageway. "When I bought the place, I had this tunnel extended."

"Where will it take us?"

Charn smiled over his shoulder. "Under the freeway to a private beach," he said. "I keep a boat there. By the time anyone realizes we're missing, we'll be halfway to San Francisco."

THE LOCAL LAW ENFORCERS hadn't had a busier day since the bootleg busts of the Prohibition. In addition to the persistent drone of police helicopters, sirens announced the clamoring approach of ground reinforcements, many of them men who'd answered APBs earlier at Lanschel Landing and San Luis Obispo. In the face of so large a show of force, only a few of Widdar Charn's men continued to wage a defense of their assigned turf, rattling guns at the choppers and scouring the grounds around the blazing barn for signs of intruders. The others, however, had already given up the fight and were dashing madly through the vineyards in hopes of escaping the dragnet they felt closing in on them.

In the ensuing chaos Bolan was able to steal his way closer to the mansion without exchanging fire with any more of the enemy. Once he reached a supply shed next to the main distillery, he paused to catch his breath and evaluate the situation.

The sheer number of gunmen and their likely link to Prince Widdar Charn made it a certainty that there was more going on at the estate than the making of wine. It seemed equally certain that inside the mansion Bolan might find not only Charn but also some incriminating evidence that might shed light on Charn's role in the smuggling operation and how the renegade Mertardans planned to strike against the pipeline. Bolan had the option of waiting for the other authorities before storming the mansion, but he was wary of giving Charn a chance to destroy evidence or attempt an escape. In his mind there was only one acceptable course of action.

Bolan used his button mike to contact Grimaldi in one of the choppers. He passed along the news about Charn's involvement in the conspiracy, then concluded, "Keep drawing fire away from the mansion. I'm going to try to slip in."

Gun in hand, Bolan ventured into the orange orchard, where the evenly spaced trees afforded reasonable cover, although twice he had to veer off the main path and conceal himself against the approach of armed guards rushing from the mansion to investigate the chaos in the fields.

Clearing the grove, he came upon a seven-car garage. Half the bay doors were open, and Bolan was heartened by the sight of several high-priced luxury cars and a white stretch limo. Hopefully it meant that Charn and other key figures hadn't had a chance to flee the mansion yet. Wanting to make sure it stayed that way, Bolan slipped into the structure, switched his Desert Eagle to his left hand and once again unsheathed his knife. As he moved from car to car, the sharp, sturdy blade easily pierced through steel-belted sidewalls, causing irreparable damage and immobilizing the vehicles.

Withdrawing the knife from the last flattened tire on the limousine, the warrior turned his attention to a door in the back of the garage. Having scanned the layout of the grounds during his approach, he knew the door led to a passageway linking the garage to the mansion. He started toward it.

Suddenly the limo's driver door swung open, slamming into Bolan and knocking the .44 from his hand. He staggered with the impact, bounding off a Jaguar XKE parked next to the vehicle.

A chauffeur who'd been hiding inside the limo charged out at Bolan, brandishing a small .22-caliber pistol. The warrior lashed out with his foot, striking the other man's gun hand as he was pulling the trigger. The errant shot shattered the Jag's side window. Before the chauffeur could recover and fire again, Bolan leaned into him with an upward thrust of the survival knife. Their eyes locked briefly, and Bolan saw the man's look of shock as the blade ripped through him. Bolan pulled the knife free and shoved the man away, retrieving his Desert Eagle before advancing to the door.

Apparently used as part of vineyard tours, the windowless corridor was well lighted and lined with photos and illustrated charts depicting the wine-making process. There was a diorama halfway down the hall featuring a scaled-down replica of the winery, and as Bolan approached it, a guard rose from behind the wooden stand and fired over the tops of miniaturized trees.

Bolan dived forward, flattening himself on the carpeted walkway. Bringing his .44 into firing position, he slammed two shots into the diorama stand. As he expected, the stand was hollow, lined with quarter-inch plywood that did little to slow or divert the twin slugs. With a groan the guard slumped into view, his revolver tumbling to the carpet beside him. Bolan leaped to his feet and scrambled past.

The hallway led first to a small anteroom filled with souvenirs and other tourist knickknacks, then into the ground floor of the mansion itself, which had years ago been converted from living quarters into a visitor's center. The main room was stocked with large displays of wine, and other doorways led to the tasting room and a dining area. In sharp contrast to the raucous turmoil Bolan had encountered on the grounds, the mansion itself was eerily quiet. There was no one in the main room and a careful search of the other two chambers revealed nothing other than the fact that someone had apparently been using the tasting room before all hell had broken loose.

Bolan decided Charn and the others must have taken refuge upstairs. As he reentered the main hall, the warrior heard a scuffling sound on the huge, winding staircase that led to the upper floors. He lunged to one side, anticipating the gunfire that soon followed. Bullets smashed into a rack of premium wines behind Bolan, spilling dark, bloodlike stains into the beige carpet. From his cover inside a pantry just behind a cashier's counter, Bolan spotted a gunman crouched on the stairway landing. The two men exchanged several rounds of fire. Bolan's aim proved the better; a well-placed shot ripped through the sniper's neck, sending him tumbling down the stairs.

The Executioner was about to step out of the pantry when something caught his eye. He turned, glancing down at the base of a shelving unit holding supplies. Closer inspection revealed that a slight rise in the carpet had snagged the bottom of the shelf, keeping it from coming flush with the wall. There was a gap behind the unit, and Bolan could feel a draft of cold air seeping through an opening. He whipped out his knife and held it close to the narrow opening. Shining the hilt's light, he was able to make out the ladder rungs leading down into darkness.

"Damn!"

Bolan tried to use the blade as a lever, but no matter how much weight he applied, he wasn't able to budge the shelving unit. He wasted a few more seconds groping for a hidden switch, then decided there was only one way he was going to get into the opening.

Unclipping a grenade from his waist, Bolan quickly surveyed the room for possible cover. There was nothing in the cramped quarters that would have shielded him adequately, so he retreated to the lobby, then pulled the pin and flung the grenade back into the pantry before crouching behind the cashier's counter.

The explosion was deafening and devastating. It turned the pantry to rubble and generated shock waves that shattered even more bottles of wine in the showroom. Bolan scrambled out from behind the counter and charged through a cloud of dust into what was left of the pantry. The shelving unit had been obliterated, leaving a clear opening into the secret escape passage. Several of the top ladder rungs had come loose from the explosion, and the warrior had to make his way cautiously when he entered the cavity and began his descent. Moments later he was in the tunnel, with lights still illuminating the way to Charn's secret marina.

Bolan broke into a run, hoping to gain ground on whoever was attempting to use the tunnel as a means of escape. After more than fifty yards, there was a bend in the tunnel. He slowed to a stop and listened. Above the thumping of his heart, the Executioner could make out distant footsteps, followed by the creaking of unoiled hinges.

Rounding the corner, Bolan started down the last length of tunnel. He'd gone another fifty yards when he heard an unexpected noise. He stopped, straining his ears to confirm his suspicions.

Water.

Seconds later he could see it, a raging current of seawater surging down the tunnel toward him. There was no time for him to turn back, and no way to get out of the water's path. All he could do was brace himself, and wait....

7

"That should keep anyone from following us," Charn said as he gave the lever a final turn.

With the valve fully opened, both he and Daifreize could hear the thunderous roar of the sea as it poured into the tunnel they'd used to escape the besieged winery. They were safely out of the passageway, standing in the moonlight on a concrete platform saddling the valve. Waves crashed against the outer walls as the two men strode along a walkway overlooking a scenic stretch of coastline. A few hundred yards away there were scattered strips of private beach linked to clifftop estates by long, meandering staircases, but the rest of the shoreline was rocky and inaccessible.

"Nice setup," Daifreize remarked as they made their way in darkness, their footsteps drowned out by the pounding surf and the shrieks of the gulls flying overhead.

"Always leave yourself an out," Charn said. At the end of the walkway, the prince began leading his fellow Saudi down a series of wooden steps anchored to rock with huge bolts and nuts. "It's a philosophy my uncle taught me years ago. I've never forgotten it, and it's served me well on more than one occasion."

"I believe it." Daifreize reflexively glanced back over his shoulder to make sure they weren't being followed. Assured that they were alone, he fell back in step behind the prince, already calculating ways he could turn events to his advantage. After all, it was a rare enough opportunity to be alone with someone of Charn's clout; to be in a position to help save the prince from apprehension or worse seemed an even more valuable destiny.

The staircase eventually brought the men down to sea level. Charn's boathouse was strategically cradled between two large boulder formations that jutted into the surf like behemoth stone sentries. The rocks also served as breakers, creating a pocket of calmer water well suited to the launching of small craft. Situated twenty yards out into the cove, the boathouse was reachable by a small two-seat lift similar to those used at ski ranges.

"Get in while I start the generator," Charn said.

Daifreize climbed up and settled into one of the seats, lighting a cigarette as he watched the prince struggle with the generator's controls. Several times the machinery seemed on the verge of turning over, only to grind to an unnerving halt. Charn fumed and filled the night air with a burst of obscenities.

"Perhaps I can help," Daifreize volunteered, climbing back down from the seat. "I've worked with these things before."

"So have I!" Charn raged with increasing frustration. "But go ahead, see what you can do. And hurry!"

Even in the dark, Daifreize could see that the prince had neglected to activate the generator's spark plug. It would have been easy enough to point out the error and make the necessary correction, but given the prince's agitation, Daifreize felt it would be more prudent to do a little aimless tinkering and attribute the problem to something less obvious.

After all, Daifreize reasoned, they could afford a few extra seconds. No one was going to catch up with them at this point.

AS THE WALL OF WATER hurtled toward him, Bolan's attention was drawn to the closest of the numerous overhead light fixtures illuminating the tunnel. The fixture was recessed into the chiseled stone and held in place by a wrought-iron bracket. There were handles on either side of the bracket, and although Bolan had his doubts as to whether they'd hold his weight, they represented his best chance of survival.

He abruptly turned his back to the onrushing tide, then crouched and leaped up just as the water slammed into him. The brutal force of the icy current took hold of him at virtually the same time he grabbed hold of the bracket rungs. He closed his eyes and held his breath as the water engulfed him. He could feel himself being jerked by the flow, and the bracket at first seemed to be giving way under his weight, but he refused to relinquish his grip.

It was difficult to gauge time under such circumstances, as time seemed to drag on interminably. With his back to the current, Bolan was able to tuck his chin to his chest and steal gasps of air during those fleeting seconds when the flow dropped below his shoulders. The bracket continued to hold firm, as did the handles.

He held on, fighting for each needed breath and focusing on the image of his fingers curled tightly around the bracket rungs. Meanwhile numbness began to creep down his arms and up his legs. Nature in its most elemental form was slowly asserting its dominance, and Bolan knew that no matter how much willpower he exerted, without some kind of intervention, this was a battle he was destined to lose.

Then, just as the chill was on the verge of pulling him into the black void of unconsciousness, Bolan was surprised to draw in one stolen breath and realize that he was able to take a second immediately afterward. Was it possible that the water level had dropped below his shoulders? He opened his eyes and saw that the depth was indeed lowering by the second.

The force of the current was lessening proportionately, and when Bolan finally let go of the rungs, he dropped with a resounding splash to the tunnel floor and was dragged along only a few yards before he was able to rise to his feet and hold his ground. The water was now less than waist deep.

Keep moving, Bolan told himself as he waded through the dark waters. After a point, the river stayed calf deep, showing no signs of lowering any farther. As he slogged onward, the warrior could hear a strange sound, part gurgling, part hiss. Reaching the end of the tunnel, his gaze fell on the opened valve, which had become so clogged with thick buildups of kelp and driftwood that only a faint trickle of ocean water was still seeping through. Mustering his strength, Bolan wrestled the valve closed, then lumbered up the short flight of steps that took him from the tunnel to the outer walkway.

The ocean breeze made the Executioner feel even colder as he stood in the open, briefly exulting at having once more cheated the Reaper.

At the sound of a motor groaning to life in the distance, he glanced to his right and spotted Charn's boathouse. When he saw two figures scrambling onto a lift, he broke into a painful jog. There was still little sensation in his legs, and Bolan had to take care that he didn't accidentally turn an ankle or otherwise throw himself off balance, as it was only a short drop to the tidewaters that pounded fiercely at the base of the walkway.

By the time Bolan reached the staircase, the two men had reached the boathouse and were climbing down from their lift seats. One strode to the nearest door and began pressing numbers on a keypad mounted on the wall while the other remained on the outer deck.

Bolan crouched over as he started down the steps, trying not to draw attention to himself. He only made it as far as the first landing, however, before he was spotted. The man on the boathouse deck leveled a gun at him and fired.

Even as he was vaulting over the staircase railing and bracing himself to land in the wet, hard-packed sand, Bolan visually matched the man's stance with that of the assailant who'd fired at him back at the cliffs of Lanschel Landing.

He knew it was the same man.

Bolan had lost both of his guns, and he was too far from the boathouse to have any use for his knife. That left only his grenades, and he was down to his last one, having lost the rest back in the tunnel. Inching through the sand, he made his way around a dune that provided visual cover from the gunman on the deck. When he felt that he was within throwing range, Bolan grappled with the pin, trying to get his numbed fingers to respond to his mental commands. Once the pin was out, he struggled to his feet and whipped his arm around, letting the deadly bomb fly....

SEEING THE GRENADE flying toward him, Daifreize flinched, throwing his aim off just enough to miss drilling the Executioner through the chest. His shot went wide and was lost in the sand. Rather than fire again, the Saudi threw himself to the deck and placed his hands behind the back of his head to shield himself against an anticipated shower of shrapnel.

Hindered by the numbness in Bolan's arm, however, the throw fell well short of the boathouse deck, exploding loudly but harmlessly above the cresting waves. Daifreize quickly bounded back to his feet and took aim once again over the railing. Behind him, he could hear the throaty roar of the speedboat coming to life inside the boathouse.

The shoreline was dark. Daifreize peered intently for any glimpse of movement, but Bolan had taken cover and wasn't about to betray his position.

"Bastard!" Daifreize hissed into the wind. His anger was initially directed at Bolan, but when he heard the speedboat's throttle revving, Daifreize felt a sudden flash of paranoia and raced to check on the prince. Jerking open the side door, he entered the boathouse just as Charn was tugging the last mooring line inside the boat. The two men's eyes met briefly, and Daifreize knew in an instant that the prince had intended to leave without him. It was only when Charn's gaze shifted briefly to the gun in Daifreize's hand that he appeared ready to consider another plan.

"Get in!" the prince called. "I was waiting for you. What happened out there?"

Daifreize briefly considered putting a hole through the prince's forehead, but thought better of it and lowered the gun as he jumped down into the boat. "Somebody just wanted to give us a little send-off."

"And you took care of him?"

Daifreize evaded the question, instead pointing out where the main door of the boathouse had been raised to provide an avenue for escape. "Let's get out of here."

The speedboat was a state-of-the-art twin-engine Cogzal, packing sufficient horsepower to jolt from the boathouse like a rodeo bull leaving the gate. Uncontested, Charn guided the boat through the choppy surf and out to sea, slowly building more speed in the event it became necessary to outrun any Coast Guard vehicle that might take up the chase.

As they headed farther from the shore, both men stole glances behind them and were able to see rising smoke and the floating lights of helicopters hovering above the beleaguered winery.

"That was close," Charn commented.

"I'll say. Odds are they're going to figure out it's your vineyard, you know."

"Perhaps," Charn conceded. "But once we've achieved our objective, it won't matter."

"We're going to have to push up the timetable," Daifreize said. "We have to get the Mertardans into the country and up to Alaska before the authorities have a chance to act on whatever they might find out from prisoners."

"It shall be done," Charn assured Daifreize. "You needn't worry."

"I'm not worried," Daifreize snapped, recalling a similar response he'd made to one of the prince's laborers at the bonfire earlier that evening.

Both men fell silent for some time. Their course took them far out into the ocean, to a point where only the thinnest ribbon of land remained visible on the coastal horizon. Charn concentrated for the most part on navigating his craft through the rough waters. Daifreize, in turn, discreetly kept an eye on the prince, committing to memory those few maneuvers that made handling the Cogzal different from any of the several dozen other boats he'd handled over the years. Once he felt confident that he could handle this boat as well, he took action on what he'd wanted to do since he'd first caught the prince trying to leave the mainland without him.

Unholstering his Browning semiautomatic, Daifreize jabbed the gun into Charn's side.

"So, tell me, O great Prince... when did you decide I was, shall we say, expendable?"

"What?" Charn gasped, instinctively raising his hands to his sides in a gesture of surrender. With the throttle untended, the boat began to slow down. "What is the meaning of this?"

"I think they call it mutiny," Daifreize said calmly as he frisked the prince, coming up with the microcassette of Darvin's plan for smuggling the Mertardans into the States and a palm-size derringer tucked in Charn's boot. Daifreize pocketed the weapon, then suddenly lashed out, pistol-whipping Charn across the face. The prince screamed in pain as he reeled backward into the side railing.

"Ehki!" Charn pleaded as he dabbed at the blood trickling from the corner of his mouth. "You're making a mistake!"

"I don't think so."

Daifreize nonchalantly pumped four shots into the other man. Dumbfounded, Charn took the hits without moving, and as he slumped to the floorboards of the boat, he stared up at his murderer with fear and horror.

"Please," he begged. "No—"

"It's done." Daifreize fired a last shot into Charn's face. "You see, dear Prince, you misjudged the situation. It's you who is dispensable."

As if to prove it, Daifreize took a step forward and seized the dead prince's arms. With some doing, he was able to fling the man up across the boat's railing, then over and into the water. The corpse splashed loudly and slipped beneath the waves.

Daifreize paused to light a cigarette, then took his place behind the boat's controls. Sure, he was going to owe Sheikh Leih Baibdi an explanation about his nephew, but Daifreize was sure he could manage that, especially if he was able to couple the news with word that he'd succeeded in bringing the Mertardans into the country and arranging for them to strike their target.

"I'll be sitting on top of the world," Daifreize said to himself as he sped through the night.

8

It was shortly after dawn. A dry sauna helped thaw the last bit of chill in Mack Bolan's bones. He sat hunched over on a wooden bench, towel draped around his waist, eyes focused vaguely on the glowing bed of hot rocks on the other side of the small room. He was in a dark mood. Some of it was attributable to fatigue. He'd had a few hours of sleep after being picked up on the beach by Grimaldi's chopper after the raid on Whitson-Drew Vineyards, but after the beating his body had taken the previous day he'd need more than a catnap to feel fully restored. Now that it seemed his next destination would be Alaska, there'd be a long plane ride during which he could recoup his strength. He was sure he'd be needing it.

Beyond a sense of exhaustion, though, Bolan's funk was also due to having seen a foe elude his grasp, not once, but twice in the same day. Sure, both Grimaldi and Brognola had pointed out that Bolan was vastly outnumbered in both instances and should consider himself lucky at merely having survived, but for a man who always expected positive results, there could be no adequate excuse for letting this one get away.

There was a tall ceramic mug of hot soup cradled in Bolan's palms. He drained it, then, in a sudden fit of frustration, he flung it against the wall. The mug shattered loudly to the floor. As Bolan rose from the bench and started out the door, he saw Brognola rushing in from an adjacent room, his avuncular face etched with concern.

"Mack, are you all right?"

"Yeah," Bolan muttered, grabbing a bathrobe from a hook behind the door and throwing it on. "Yeah, I'm doing just great."

Bolan, Brognola and Grimaldi were cloistered in one of the back cabins at Varkes Hollow, a popular upscale retreat located a few miles outside of San Luis Obispo. Through an open window, Bolan could see the first light working its way through the thick canopy of ancient evergreens crowding the grounds. There was a pine scent to the fire blazing in the hearth when Bolan and Brognola entered the main room. Grimaldi was seated at a table with Mookie Sandhoff, the FBI photo expert. They glanced up from a pile of glossies spread out before them.

"Morning, Sunshine," Grimaldi called out to Bolan with a broad grin. The Executioner frowned at Grimaldi a moment, then let his features soften as he grabbed a breakfast roll from the kitchen counter.

"Okay." Bolan sighed. "Where do we stand?"

Brognola brought the big guy up to date.

"We took a few prisoners at the winery and got a couple of them to talk. Apparently Prince Widdar Charn is the shadow owner of the place, and he had it staffed with a lot of Saudi loyalists with bogus Mexican visas."

"Why?"

"We aren't sure at this point," Brognola confessed, "but obviously he wanted it to look like just another typical California vineyard. They ran a good front, too. Reports we got our hands on say most of their wines get good ratings, and they were turning a handsome profit. It might just be that Charn wanted the place as an investment."

Bolan shook his head. "Not with the kind of firepower he had stockpiled there. I don't buy it."

"Well," the big Fed went on, "we had two different prisoners both tell us that they only brought in munitions a couple months ago."

"About the same time the Feds started closing in on Stasha Darvin," Mookie commented.

"Exactly," Brognola confirmed. "So my guess is that either Charn wanted to have a backup force for the Mertardans once they were in the country, or else he was planning some other operation down the line."

Bolan ate the roll and washed it down with fresh coffee as he wandered to the table and eyed some of the photos Mookie and Grimaldi had been looking at. There were blowups of the shots José Markrey had taken at Lanschel Landing, as well as mug shots culled from the Bureau's rogue gallery of known international terrorists.

"No matchups yet," Grimaldi said, guessing Bolan's next question. "Seems like they were smart enough to use people not on file anywhere."

"Including him?" Bolan asked, pointing at one of the blowups of the man in the blue sweats.

"Affirmative," Grimaldi said. "And none of the people we captured claims to know him, either."

"We do have one lead on that front, though," Brognola said. He joined the others at the table and pointed to two of the figures in Markrey's photo of the Chrysler Imperial. "One of these guys you plugged in San Luis Obispo, and the other we found buried in a shallow grave out by the vineyards. Neither had any papers on them and their prints haven't rung any bells yet, but from the looks of them, I'd say they're brothers. That might help."

"Maybe." Bolan glanced back at the man in the blue sweats. "What about him and the prince? Did they get away?"

Brognola sighed and withdrew one of his trademark cigars from his shirt pocket. He nodded wearily as he fussed with the wrapper. "We've had the Coast Guard and three other agencies combing the coast in both directions, but there's no trace of either them or their boat. Sorry, Striker."

"Well, the odds are they'll turn up in Alaska, right?" Bolan speculated.

"That depends," the head Fed replied. "The pipeline may be the ultimate target, but we have no confirmation through our intel that the Mertardans are in the country yet. It might be that they're going to be brought in somewhere else besides Alaska. Charn and this other guy might be headed there."

A phone clanged in the background. Brognola excused himself to answer it.

As the Executioner finished his coffee, he looked over a map of California laid out amid the photos on the table. With so much coastline, there could be any number of places where the missing speedboat might have been brought ashore and hidden during the night. And, as with any search for criminals at large, the more time that elapsed, the less likelihood there'd be of bringing the men in. He figured it'd be best to leave that part of the operation to the Coast Guard and other agencies. By the same token he doubted that he'd be put to his best use trying to figure out where the terrorists were going to be brought into the country. Given the way things were playing out, it made more sense to jump to the worst possible scenario and assume the Mertardans were already in the States, or that they'd slip in before anyone could discover their point of entry. That left one clear strategy.

"I think our best shot is to get up to Alaska and try to figure which stretch of the pipeline the Mertardans are most likely to strike," Bolan told the others. "Once we do that we can backtrack and try to intercept them."

"I think you're right," Mookie said. "I've got a few contacts up that way, matter of fact. If you can handle an old fart dogging your heels, I'd like to tag along."

"Glad to have you," Bolan assured the older man.

In the background Brognola slowly hung up the phone. He pulled his cigar from its wrapper and clipped one end before slipping it between his teeth. As was his custom, he refrained from lighting up.

"Who was that?" Grimaldi asked.

"Coast Guard. They found Widdar Charn's body washed ashore about seven miles from here. Took a few rounds of 9 mm, execution-style."

"Whoa," Grimaldi muttered. "I wasn't counting on that, not by a long shot."

"Me, neither," Mookie admitted. "My money was on him being the brains behind this whole thing."

"That was my feeling, too," Brognola said. "But it looks like we're going to have to rethink that now."

Bolan picked up the telephoto shot of the man in the blue sweats. There could be little question that he was the prince's killer. But had he offed Charn of his own accord, or was he still acting on someone else's orders? One way or another, Bolan was determined to find out.

EHKI DAIFREIZE MANEUVERED the Cogzal up the narrow mouth of the Corlack River, keeping his eyes trained on both embankments for signs of activity. His Browning was tucked inside the yellow rain slicker he'd donned over his Western wear, and his hair, instead of being slicked back, was now a loose tangle falling haphazardly about his head.

He was in the heart of Big Sur, a largely pristine parcel of California coastal wilderness that over the years had captured the hearts and imaginations of artists as diverse as Henry Miller and Ansel Adams. Redwoods and chaparral grew abundantly, not only within the confines of the eight-hundred-acre state park, but also on those discreetly carved-out plots of land maintained by the area's meager population of one thousand.

Daifreize had boated his way north during the night, eluding search teams through a combination of deft handling and pure luck. He considered himself fortunate to have gotten this far undetected and wasn't about to tempt fate by spending much more time in Charn's boat.

He was rounding a bend in the river when he heard the bleating thump of an approaching helicopter. Killing the motor, Daifreize nudged the prow of the boat into the loamy embrace of the closest riverbank. Reaching up, he grabbed hold of an evergreen growing at the stream's edge and gently pulled the limb closer to provide a fuller screen against being seen from overhead. With his other hand he pulled out his semiautomatic.

Daifreize caught a brief glimpse of the chopper as it drifted overhead, apparently following the river back out to the ocean. The craft made no pretense at slowing down after passing above the speedboat, and the Saudi exhaled with relief as he lowered his gun. He was about to restart the motor and continue downriver when he heard a rustling in the brush behind him. Whirling, he saw an old man making his way down a dirt path leading to the river's edge, dressed in hip boots and a weathered windbreaker. He was carrying a fishing rod and tackle box, and puffing contentedly on a corncob pipe.

Daifreize hastened to slip his gun back inside his coat before he was spotted, but he was too late. As the fisherman happened to glance up, his eyes narrowed at the sight of the gleaming Browning.

"See here now!" the old man bristled. "Can't you read signs? There's no hunting in these parts! None! Do you hear?"

"Sorry, old-timer," Daifreize said, taking aim at the fisherman's chest. "You shouldn't have come here."

One shot was all that was needed to kill the man. Taking the slug under his right eye, the fisherman keeled to one side, dropping both his rod and tackle box. The strap to his hip boots snagged on a tree, propping him up at a bizarre angle so that he was half in the river, half out. Blood tinged the river around him red.

Daifreize quickly lashed the Cogzal to a tree and bounded ashore. Twenty yards upstream was a pedestrian bridge that spanned the river. He crossed over, then quickly backtracked to the body. Leaning out over the water, he carefully pulled the man's wallet from his vest and pocketed it. Next he stuffed rocks down the man's hip boots, then untangled him from the tree. Weighed down, the fisherman slipped quickly below the waterline and was soon barely visible at the bottom of the river.

A quick inspection of the dead man's wallet revealed that he lived in Big Sur. The dirt path the old man had taken to the river wound its way up to a modest one-story cottage nestled in the trees. Propped on the roof were two antennae, one a satellite dish for television reception, the other the type used by ham-radio buffs for transmitting and receiving global messages. Daifreize smiled to himself. The radio in the speedboat hadn't been powerful enough to serve his plans, but he suspected the unit inside the house would be another matter.

He deduced that the dead man lived in the cottage, and judging from the size of the house, it seemed likely he either lived alone or with only one other person.

There was one way to find out for sure.

Halfway up the path, Daifreize heard the deep-throated warning growl of a huge mastiff lying on the front porch of the cottage. As the dog rose to its feet and began to bark with louder insistence, Daifreize stood still and steadied his aim. It took two shots to silence the animal. Daifreize rushed forward and circled the cottage. Prepared to fire again if need be, he peered into one of the windows. The house seemed empty.

The window was locked shut. Daifreize went around back and found the rear door unlocked. He entered the cottage and quickly searched its three rooms, confirming that the fisherman was its lone occupant. There was an old tin coffee percolator resting atop a Franklin stove in the kitchen area. The Saudi helped himself to a cup and raided the pantry for a handful of buttermilk biscuits. He stuffed one in his mouth and chewed it as he crossed the room.

The radio was set on a large table near a picture window that provided a magnificent view of the ocean. Daifreize sat before the controls, flicking switches and dials between bites of his biscuit. He was grateful that he was gifted with a good memory, because there was no machine in the cottage to play back the microcassette. He had to rely on his own recollections of the meeting with Darvin to recall the right frequencies and codes to put himself in touch with the people who would have helped Darvin smuggle the Mertardans into the States.

It took a little over half an hour to make the necessary contacts, after which time the gears were put into motion. Barring any unforeseen problems, the Mertardans would be in the country and bound for Alaska by the end of the day.

"And so will I," Daifreize whispered to himself as he finished the last of the coffee. "So will I."

9

Emerging through a bank of low-hanging clouds that had just finished powdering the nearby mountaintops with fresh snow, a chartered Lear jet set down on a remote airfield two miles north of Valdez. By the time the plane jockeyed to a stop near a small hangar at the far end of the runway, a Jeep had wandered onto the tarmac and made its way over for a rendezvous.

Mookie Sandhoff was the first man out of the plane, followed by Mack Bolan and Jack Grimaldi. The flight had been thankfully uneventful, giving them all a chance to sleep. Bolan in particular looked revitalized, ready for whatever the next phase of this mission might call for.

Sandhoff handled introductions when the man in the Jeep got out to meet them.

"Guys," he said, "this is my old frat buddy, Deton Smith."

A tall, lean man with a flattened nose testifying to a brief stint on the amateur boxing circuit, Smith was head of internal security for the Department of National Resources, the government agency in charge of

ensuring pipeline safety and overseeing the multibil-
lion-dollar operation that had been bringing oil down
from the North Slope reservoirs for nearly fifteen
years. During that time, the greatest foes Smith had
had to deal with were inept bureaucrats and unscru-
pulous construction firms cutting corners to make
deadlines and maximize profits. Now that it looked as
if there was a more blatant and malevolent threat to
contend with, Smith was glad that he was among the
first to be notified.

"C'mon inside," Smith told the others, motioning
them toward the hangar. "I figured it'd be a good idea
if we got as many heads together on this as possible,
so I called in a couple more people."

As they walked behind the others, Bolan and Grimaldi exchanged wary glances. Thus far this entire
operation had been dogged by bureaucratic overkill,
and both men had taken consolation in the hope that
the remoteness of the pipeline would weed out the excess baggage. Now it looked as if even the more forbidding elements of Alaska were no deterrent to the
inevitability of red tape.

In addition to serving as a transport hub for the
DNR, the state-owned hangar had been recently ren-
ovated to include a second-story suite that housed field
offices for Ranton Oil, the conglomerates of seven
major oil producers charged with running the pipeline, as well as a handful of other state agencies with
a stake in pipeline-related activities. Smith had called
ahead before setting out from his home in downtown

Valdez, and when the men entered a second-story conference room, there were three others waiting for them.

Greg Miffee, a boyishly handsome man with the build of an NFL linebacker, represented All-Laska Technological Services, which handled most inspections and repairs of the pipeline, both in terms of the existing line and all materials brought to any of the three dozen workstations situated along the line's rambling route.

Seated next to him was Ranton Oil's vice president of operations, Rafael Anpard. A short, mustached man wearing a tan blazer and white turtleneck, Anpard's casual dress was offset by his no-nonsense demeanor. Never one to waste a moment of work, he was busily putting together figures for a meeting scheduled later that morning and barely looked up from his calculator when the men entered.

The third person was Michelle Raineswell, an Aleut Indian in her early thirties. She served as liaison for the Alaskan Native Council, a political consortium representing the state's various Indian tribes in matters ranging from negotiation of mineral rights on Indian lands to hiring practices for local workers.

"Okay, we've got a lot of work to do, so I'll be quick with introductions," Smith said. True to his word, he haphazardly gestured around the room as he rattled off names.

When Bolan was introduced to Raineswell, he couldn't help but be struck by the woman's well-sculpted features and the self-assuredness of her gaze.

"Pleased to meet you, Mr. Belasko," she said with a warm smile as they shook hands.

"Likewise," Bolan replied. Michelle's gaze lingered on him a moment longer, then shifted to her delicate hands.

Once introductions were completed, Deton Smith took charge of the meeting, briefing Anpard, Raineswell and Miffee on the incidents in Cinnaton and San Luis Obispo that had led to the current state of crisis alert.

"And so, at this point," he concluded, "I think we have two priority matters to concern ourselves with. First we need to take a long, hard look at the pipeline and try to calculate the weakest links in terms of vulnerability to a terrorist attack. And secondly we need to be concerned with the possibility that these Mertardans and whomever they've allied with have established some kind of rapport with individuals associated with the pipeline."

"Moles?" Miffee asked.

"I'm afraid so."

Anpard took his hand off his calculator for the first time since the meeting had begun. "You're accusing our people of conspiring with some Middle East nut cases?"

"Not necessarily," Mookie Sandhoff speculated. "I mean, there are a lot of hands in the pipeline pie besides yours."

"That's for sure," Anpard snarled, making little effort to disguise his disdain for most of the others in the room. "It's amazing how many people with no pipeline experience seem to think they know how to do our job better than we do."

"Let's not get into that now, Raffi, okay?" Michelle implored. "This problem goes beyond politics. We all stand to lose here."

"Exactly," Smith agreed.

"Okay, fine," Anpard said with a shrug. "I just don't see where you come off assuming these people have someone on the inside."

"Easy," Mookie replied. "Think about it a minute. The Mertardans are being smuggled into the country at a big risk, and not just so they can wander up here in snowmobiles and lob a few random grenades in hopes they might cause some damage."

"Mookie's right," Bolan said. "We've gone over their modus operandi on the attacks they made on our bases in the Persian Gulf, and in each instance it was clear that they'd done their homework and figured out the way to cause the most damage with the least risk to themselves. In terms of the pipeline, we have to assume they have access to flowcharts, design specs, even details on guard shifts and times of aerial surveillance."

"One thing's for sure," Anpard said. "They've picked one hell of a time to throw a monkey wrench at us."

"How so?" Grimaldi asked.

"Well, we're in the process of trying to come up to full capacity," the Ranton executive explained. "Once we get the green light, we go to 2.1 million barrels a day, and that's going to mean full pressure on the pipeline, which means—"

"Which means," Michelle interjected, "that if there's sabotage we're going to have oil gushing out like a geyser, probably on Native land."

"Look who's getting political now," Anpard sniped. "And for the record, I'm sure you know just like everyone else here that we have safety valves located the entire length of the pipeline. Any breakage and the line shuts down. The most you'll ever see spilling is a few thousand gallons."

"Unless the Mertardans have learned a way to foul the safety lines," Bolan suggested.

"Totally impossible," Anpard insisted. "It just doesn't work that way."

"Word was that our Persian Gulf bases were totally impregnable to terrorist assault, too," Bolan reminded Anpard. "Look what happened there."

"A completely different situation. There you're dealing with Pentagon hype. I'm saying it's a physical impossibility to sever the pipeline at any point without the flow being shut off before there's widespread damage."

"If you say so." Bolan didn't sound convinced, however.

"You're painting a pretty bleak picture, Mr. Belasko," Michelle said.

"Just trying to be realistic. The best chance we've got here is to brace ourselves for the worst and pull out all the stops."

There was a relief map of Alaska mounted on the wall. Greg Miffee rose from his chair and approached. "Well, we can go over a lot of data and whatnot to try to calculate the most vulnerable stretch of pipeline, but I get the idea we can't afford to waste time on a lot of paper chasing."

"That's right," Bolan told him. "We have some people crunching numbers back East, but we're looking for a more immediate strategy."

"Gut calls, eh?" Miffee extended his arm and pointed to the northernmost stretch of the pipeline. "Well, there's no question but that we're most vulnerable to attack up here, between Deadhorse and Ray River. You want to narrow it down even more, I'd say concentrate on the North Slope, just above Brooks Range. It's real no-man's-land out there. Arctic conditions, hardly any roads, minimum security... And on top of all that, we've probably had more problems with pipe there than anywhere else."

"Is that right?" Bolan asked the others.

Raineswell and Smith nodded.

"It's a fair assessment," Anpard conceded. "But a lot of the problems were due to a shipment of faulty materials from foreign suppliers. Since we replaced those, things have been running much smoother."

"Granted," Smith said, "but Greg's right. Weigh in all the other variables and it's still the likeliest target."

"And we're still talking about a hundred-mile stretch," Miffee said. "And that doesn't include any of the surrounding area. Seems like we have to take that into consideration, too."

Bolan nodded. "Fine. Then I say we wrap this up as quickly as possible so we can get up there, pronto."

Over the next half hour a quick battle plan was drawn. Bolan, Grimaldi and Sandhoff would handle aerial surveillance in one of the DNR's jets. Smith and Miffee would fly up separately and round up a ground force of several dogsled and snowmobile crews to visually inspect the pipeline for signs that unauthorized individuals had been in the area. Raineswell and Anpard, meanwhile, would concentrate on checking the ranks of Ranton employees and pipeline workers, both union and free-lance, in hopes of unearthing the suspected traitors thought to be aiding the Mertardans in their plans to sabotage the pipeline.

"Good luck," Bolan told Michelle as they left the conference room at the meeting's end.

"Thanks," she told him with a rueful smile. "I'm going to need it. I can't think of a more unpleasant task than having to face your own people with the idea that one of them is out to stab you in the back."

"I know. A part of you feels ashamed at having a lack of faith, but then another part feels as if you've been personally violated by their deceit."

"Yes," she said, "that's it exactly."

They continued to talk together as they walked with the others down the steps to the main chamber of the hangar. Mechanics were out in full force, working on two choppers and three different planes. A back door led out to a parking lot. As Bolan walked Michelle to her car, she asked him, "Maybe you'd be interested in dinner before you head out? I know the best place in Valdez to have fresh fish, and the view is just spectacular."

"Thanks," Bolan said with a tinge of regret, "but we're going to be on our way as soon as we can clear the paperwork and fuel up a plane."

"That's too bad."

"Maybe I'll take a rain check," Bolan suggested.

"Okay, and I'm holding you to it, Mr. Belasko."

They shook hands, then Bolan held the door open as she got in behind the wheel. Once she had the engine started, he closed the door and waved to her, then backtracked to the hangar, where Grimaldi was conferring with one of the mechanics.

"Excuse me a second," Grimaldi told the other man. He moved away and followed Bolan to a workbench a few yards away.

"We're clear to go?" the warrior asked.

"Yeah, no problem," Grimaldi said. With a wink, he added, "And what about you?"

Bolan cocked an inquiring eyebrow.

"It looked like Ms. Raineswell was giving you an okay for liftoff herself."

"You're dreaming, Jack." Bolan gestured toward the mechanic. "Just get us some wings so we can get out of here."

"Sure, sure," Grimaldi said. "But take my word . . . you can run but you can't hide."

Bolan shook his head and started back up the steps to track down Mookie Sandhoff.

FOR WEEKS the authorities had been monitoring Stasha Darvin's rug-import business in hopes of turning up the means by which the man had hoped to smuggle the Mertardan terrorists into the country. To their increasing frustration, however, Darvin's entire operation continued to go strictly by the book, avoiding even the smallest infractions that nearly every importer or exporter was guilty of attempting at one time or another. In fact, prior to his death Darvin had cut off all ties with the two international firms whose activities had put the Feds on his scent in the first place. Paradoxically, the more zealously Darvin's people adhered to the letter of the law, even after his death, the greater the suspicions that the clean facade was a cover for clandestine dirty dealings.

After the siege of Whitson-Drew Vineyards, additional manpower was brought in to investigate the winery, not only in terms of its on-site operations, but also its other dealings, particularly in terms of supply vendors and high-volume clientele. The hope was that somehow the link between Darvin and the winery would prove to be the key to apprehending the Mertardans.

Ultimately, however, all such queries would prove fruitless, empty-handed, serving only to stray investigators from stumbling onto a peripheral network of little-known friends and acquaintances Darvin had accumulated over the years. It was through these contacts that Darvin proposed to smuggle the terrorists into the country, not in one readily identifiable group but in small groups of between one and three men.

Two of the Mertardans, for instance, gained admittance by concealing themselves in large pieces of machinery being shipped to Anchorage by a supply firm owned by the brother-in-law of one of Darvin's clients in Oakland. Darvin had befriended the man during a high-stakes poker game more than two years earlier, then gradually cultivated an informal friendship, waiting until last week to call in his marker and ask the man a favor.

Another terrorist had strolled freely off a plane in Vancouver and been chauffeured northward under the guise of being a diplomatic courier. All the necessary falsified papers had been put into order by another of Darvin's seemingly casual acquaintances, a print master in the Dominican Republic who also happened to be a top-notch weaver who'd handled a few special orders to repair antique rugs for some of Darvin's clients. Darvin had put the weaver's son up at his

San Luis Obispo home the previous year when the boy had taken an offer to play pro ball for the San José Bees. The grateful father had pledged that no favor would be too great to grant in return for the Iranian's generosity. Darvin had dismissed any thought of repayment . . . until last week.

And so it was under several other equally oblique connections and elaborate ruses that the other Mertardans were brought into the country. Some had already been smuggled in before Darvin's ill-fated rendezvous with Ehki Daifreize, and Daifreize had orchestrated the other maneuverings from the Big Sur cottage owned by the fisherman he'd killed and buried in the bed of the Corlack River.

Once he was sure that all the Mertardans were bound for the States and squared away as to where they were to reunite once they all reached Alaska, Daifreize had donned some of the dead fisherman's clothes and stolen his car, driving north along Highway One to San Francisco International Airport. He ditched the car and took a red-eye flight to Anchorage. He arrived before any of the terrorists, which suited him fine, as he had some other business to attend to.

At the same time Bolan and the others were conferring at the state-owned hangar outside Valdez, Daifreize was sitting on a bench across from the polar bear exhibit at Alaska Zoo, seven and a half miles south of downtown Anchorage. It was feeding time, and as a crowd gathered around the trainer and his buckets of freshly killed fish and raw meat, Daifreize nonchalantly feasted on a less exotic fare of salted peanuts and watered-down root beer.

Seated with him were two men, both wearing leather jackets. Tom Dinic, the older of the two, was one of the first wave of countless Texan immigrants who had ventured north during the initial phase of construction of the Alaskan pipeline fifteen years before. The high wages and frontier atmosphere had appealed to him immediately, and he'd been on the Ranton Oil payroll ever since, at least until his abrupt firing a month earlier. Like Roger Permensen, the man with him, he'd run afoul of the union in Tolnera, a small town on the North Slope that was essentially a work camp for Ranton Oil employees tending to the northernmost stretch of the pipeline. Both Dinic and Permensen had been found guilty of drug peddling and bilking fellow workers out of wages in rigged poker games, and in addition to being bounced from the union, they'd been banished from Tolnera, as well.

Tolnera, as it happened, was the closest workstation to the same weak links in the pipeline near Brooks Range that were presently the focus of those meeting at the air hangar in Valdez. Not surprisingly, therefore, it was to Dinic and Permensen that Ehki Daifreize had turned for laying the groundwork for the Mertardan bomb squad.

"And I just want you to take a quick run up there and double-check things," Daifreize said as he discreetly slipped each man a thick envelope filled with money and several inspection reports on the structural integrity of the North Slope pipeline. "You don't have to show your faces at the work camp. Just work around the security patrols and take a good look at the pipe along the stretches I marked down. Try to find out which ones have deteriorated the most since these last reports."

"That's it?" Dinic inquired.

"That's it. I don't need to tell you that it's in your best interests not to be caught and not to let on who's paying you."

"We don't aim to get caught." Dinic laughed. "Not when we've got another fifty grand coming."

Permensen slipped his envelope inside his coat. "I can't help but wonder," he told Daifreize, "what's your angle on this? What are you up to?"

"You aren't being paid to wonder," the Saudi reminded both men. "You have a job to do. Do it right, and you'll get the rest of your money by the end of the week."

Dinic pocketed his envelope and stood. "Sounds fair to me. Come on, cowboy," he told Permensen. "We got ourselves a plane to catch."

The two men wandered into the crowd, leaving Daifreize alone on the bench. He remained there a few minutes longer, flipping through a zoo brochure and pretending to be interested in an explanation of migration patterns of the caribou.

At half past the hour, Daifreize quickly wolfed down the last few peanuts and rinsed his mouth out with the soda, then carefully crumpled the wrapper and wax-paper cup as he rose from the bench. As he approached the nearest trash receptacle, he saw a tall, stocky man in dark jeans and an insulated windbreaker already standing there, peeling the paper off a chocolate bar. He looked harmless enough, but Daifreize recognized the man as Ruiz Kalas, hatchet man for Sheikh Leih Baibdi, who'd been dispatched to Alaska to talk with Daifreize about the unfortunate demise of Baibdi's nephew, the late Prince Widdar Charn.

"Marvelous beast, isn't it?" Kalas observed, watching one of the polar bears tear into a hunk of meat tossed into its cage.

"Yes, it certainly is."

The two men fell into step beside each other as they wandered away from the bears' den. There were countless other visitors crowding the walkway, creating a loud enough din for the men to speak freely with little concern about being overheard.

"And the caribou over there, they are quite a sight, as well," Kalas said, indicating a group of animals at a nearby feeding trough. "When one thinks of how beautiful they look here, imagine what a picture they are in their natural environment. Out there in the wild open spaces, roaming freely across unspoiled land...."

"I had no idea you were such a nature lover, Ruiz."

"Oh, I'm only like your average American citizen," the taller man said with the faintest hint of a grin. "I get all misty eyed over helpless animals. And, heaven forbid, should there be an unfortunate accident out there along that godforsaken pipeline..." He closed his eyes in mock horror and shook his head sadly.

"It would be a national tragedy," Daifreize said gravely, playing along with Kalas. "The American people would be outraged, even more than they were when that tanker ran aground in Prince William Sound."

"Oh, I should think so. They'd write their congressmen, clamor for investigations, send money to Greenpeace and their precious Sierra Club."

"Why, the pipeline would have to be closed down until everyone was sure it could be safely reopened."

"Yes, and that would take weeks, months." Kalas chuckled. "Perhaps even years."

"During which the people would still need their steady supply of oil, forcing them to look elsewhere."

"Absolutely." The men stopped halfway across a bridge spanning a marsh environment filled with a variety of ducks and geese. Daifreize took out his cigarettes and offered the pack to Kalas.

As he took one out and lighted it, Kalas said, "I'm sure my beloved Sheikh Baibdi would be able to convince his fellow OPEC members to come to the rescue of the U.S."

"Yes," Daifreize said. "For a price...."

"A very handsome price," Kalas agreed. In point of fact, both men knew the price could be well in the billions of dollars. Per week.

"The sheikh is concerned that recent events have perhaps decreased the likelihood that there will be an 'accident' along the pipeline."

Daifreize let smoke trail from his lips as he slowly shook his head. "He has no need to worry. The plan is in effect. There will be no more setbacks."

"The sheikh will be glad to hear that," Kalas said. "He has already paid a great price to see this thing happen."

"The prince's death was unfortunate," Daifreize said with feigned conviction. He'd already worked out an alibi for what had happened the previous night. "We were so close to escaping when the Americans caught up with us. I blame myself for what happened."

"You do?"

Daifreize nodded. "I was unfamiliar with the controls of the speedboat, so the prince was at the wheel when they attacked. They shot him down in cold blood, no chance to surrender, no chance to reach for his own gun. They would have slain me, too, if the prince hadn't sent me below deck to check the fuel tanks."

"I see," Kalas said calmly. "So that's how it happened?"

"I'm afraid so. The boat was still accelerating when I came up after hearing the shooting. We were too far out for them to fire at us anymore. By the same token, I had no means by which to retaliate. It was all I could do to take the controls and hope that I could figure out how to use the boat."

"Hmm." Kalas flicked his cigarette over the side of the railing. It hissed out in the marsh below. Leaning against the rail, he propped his elbows on the hand guide, then trained his eyes on Daifreize.

"A sad, touching story, Ehki," he said. "I'm sure the sheikh will believe you."

"Well, I'm sure that—"

"I don't," Kalas interrupted.

"Don't?"

"Believe you. I think you're lying through your teeth. However, I'm willing to overlook my feelings in this matter. In fact, perhaps I even sympathize with you and your position."

The men resumed walking, heading down the other side of the bridge and making their way toward the seal exhibit. By now Daifreize felt he was in Fate's hands. The fact that Kalas hadn't executed him prior to their rendezvous was indication enough that the sheikh's henchman felt he had use for him. After all this deadly small talk, most of it recounting matters that had been already discussed long ago, Daifreize finally understood the situation. Just as he'd eliminated Prince Widdar Charn as an obstruction to his own rise to power, so was Ruiz Kalas apparently setting his sights on a better life for himself after the death of Leih Baibdi, provided the sheikh could be eliminated.

"You'll see to it that the explosion goes off on schedule?" Kalas asked.

"You have my word. I've sent some men to pinpoint the best place to strike, and even as we speak the Mertardans are preparing to assemble here in Alaska. I've made arrangements to move them tomorrow up to one of the work camps. Tolnera. It's near Brooks Range. I'll be heading up there myself in the morning."

"Very good," Kalas said. "When can I expect results?"

"In two days. Three at the absolute most."

"Excellent." Kalas smiled at his colleague. "That will give me time to see to the little 'accident' *I'm* planning...."

10

To many, Alaska conjures up images of fur-clad Eskimos living out of igloos amid subzero temperatures and boundless expanses of blinding white snow. In actuality such arctic conditions comprise only a quarter of the state's nearly 400 million acres. Accordingly it wasn't until Jack Grimaldi had piloted Mack Bolan and Mookie Sandhoff nearly three-quarters of the way up the rambling Alaska Pipeline that they encountered the kind of forbidding terrain that was the stuff of Jack London adventure novels.

Brooks Range, a mountainous spine straddling the Arctic Circle, marked the beginning of the harshest stretch of land the pipeline had to traverse. Heading north, there was no relief from the barren white wilderness the rest of the way to Prudhoe Bay.

"Doesn't look like someplace I'd want to go for vacation," Grimaldi commented as he glanced out the plane's window. He was at the control of a vintage turboprop GAF Nomad 22, the pride of the DNR's limited air fleet. Bolan rode beside him in the copilot's seat while Mookie sat back near the door to the passenger compartment.

"I second that," the FBI man called out. "But at least we're up here in a climate-controlled cabin. I pity Deton and Greg."

"I think they're probably used to it by now," Bolan ventured.

"Thirty degrees below zero?" Grimaldi exclaimed. "Not counting the windchill factor? Sorry, but I doubt anybody gets used to something like that."

"The locals do," Mookie said as he stared out the window. "See down there, over to the right? Looks like a settlement."

Bolan glanced down and saw a scattering of no more than a dozen igloos and crude wooden lean-tos set up in rough half circle at the base of a small mountain. From what little background material he'd managed to go over, he suspected they were inland Eskimos, Nunamiuts or possibly Lancassos, small tribes who subsisted primarily on caribou herds roaming the range. Their settlement blended in with the surrounding environment, in sharp contrast to the pipeline more than five miles to the west, which lay primarily above the ground on an elaborate series of thick, reinforced posts intended to keep the steady flow of heated Prudhoe Bay crude oil from wreaking undue havoc on the permafrost. From the air the line looked like a long, stitched wound that was a long way from ever healing.

There was a radio mounted beneath the Nomad's control board, and since their last refueling stop in Fairbanks, Grimaldi had been trying to establish contact with Miffee and Smith.

"Air One to Dogger One, do you read?" he called into the dash mike as he veered away from the village and headed back toward a more parallel course with the pipeline. When there was no response from Greg Miffee, he put out a second call, this one to Dogger Two, Deton Smith.

"Dogger Two to Air One," came the distorted reply over the radio's small speakers. "I read."

"What's your position?"

Smith rattled off his coordinates, adding, "I'm just about two hundred yards from the Young River underpass. I think I'm on to something."

"What's that?"

"Tracks from another dogsled," Smith reported. "And it's not Miffee, either."

"One of the other search teams maybe?" Bolan speculated.

"Negative. It's unauthorized entry. I'd bet on it. Over."

"Check it out," Grimaldi told the ground patroller. "We'll swing over and do an air scan."

"Okay, I'll— Hold it!" Smith suddenly interrupted himself. "I think I see someth—"

There was a loud pop over the speaker, then Smith's voice was cut off, replaced by a steady crackle of white noise.

"What's going on?" Grimaldi said, fidgeting with the squelch controls. "Hey, Dogger Two? Do you read? Deton, are you all right?"

"Something's wrong," Sandhoff murmured.

"There was a gunshot just before we lost him," Bolan said, confirming Mookie's concern.

"Yeah, I thought it might be static, but I heard it, too," Grimaldi muttered. He continued to turn knobs on the radio, trying to tune out the white noise and home in on the voice of Deton Smith.

Mookie leaned forward, trying to forge a shred of hope. "Maybe it wasn't a gunshot," he said, gesturing at the radio's small speakers. "Listen to all that static. It could have been—"

Bolan cut in. "It was gunfire, trust me."

Grimaldi banked the plane sharply, changing course. What little excuse there was for sunlight in the midwinter sky glinted off the Nomad's struts. "Let's check it out," he said.

Bolan grabbed a pair of high-powered binoculars and peered out the window, trying to locate Miffee or any of the other dogsled teams that had set out earlier in the afternoon to inspect the pipeline for signs of tampering or vulnerability. As they drew closer to the point of Smith's last broadcast, the icy vein of Young River came into view.

Grimaldi cranked up the radio's volume. If there was any further response from Smith, it was too faint to be heard above the drone of the twin Allison 250-B17 engines flanking either side of the cockpit.

"Wind's picking up," Bolan observed, watching the fine white powder roll across the frozen ground below, creating wavelike drifts. "I can't see any tracks, and they're apt to be covered up before we get to them."

"Try to reach him again," Mookie suggested.

Bolan keyed the radio mike and spoke into it. "Air One to Dogger Two. Air One to Dogger Two, do you read?"

No answer.

"Deton, look, if you can hear me, we need your help," Bolan said. "With any luck, you've got some safety flares packed with you. Try to get to them and set one off. We'll keep circling as long as we can."

"Can't be for too long," Grimaldi said, eyeing the fuel gauge. "Tank's running low, and we've got a bit of a haul to get our buns to the nearest airfield."

"Damn right," Sandhoff called out from the back as Bolan resumed scanning with the binoculars. "Manley's a good sixty miles away."

"There!" Bolan shouted, pointing off to his right. "Tracks, and they're not from a dogsled."

"Snowmobile?" Sandhoff queried.

"Yeah," Bolan replied, "that'd be my guess. Jack, can you take us in a little closer, around two o'clock?"

"Will do."

As Grimaldi banked the plane again, Bolan panned with the binoculars, tracing the tracks in the snow. At virtually the same moment he detected a vague silhouette materializing out of the cloudy snow, there was a sudden, near-deafening thwack behind him, followed by the mad whistling of cold air rushing into the cockpit. A hole appeared in the passenger's window, and glass shattered as a bullet lodged in a storage case mounted behind the pilot's seat.

"Sniper!" Bolan shouted, reflexively dropping the binoculars and grabbing for a thick, padded mitten to plug the hole in the window. "Take her up!"

"Hold on, here we go!" Grimaldi jockeyed the controls with both hands, bringing the plane's nose up and altering its course away from the pipeline. Strapped into their seats, he and Bolan easily rolled with the sudden pitch, but Sandhoff was knocked off balance and let out a surprised yelp as he found himself slammed shoulder-first into the wall of the cockpit.

Bolan glanced back out the window. Even without the binoculars, he could now make out the distant form of someone with a rifle standing next to a snowmobile near one of the pipeline supports. The gunman was drawing a bead on the retreating plane, and although the warrior couldn't hear gunshots from inside the cockpit, he knew they were being fired on again.

"Damn!" Grimaldi gritted, eyes on the gauges as he fought with the controls. "We're losing fuel!"

"They got the tank just off to your left," Mookie told him, peering out the side window. Sure enough, a quarter-size hole had been punctured in the underside of the wing behind one of the engines.

"Great!" Grimaldi said. "That's just great!"

"Can you bring us down?" Bolan asked.

"Hell, yes. Maybe even in one piece."

"Go for it. It's our only chance."

"Amen." Grimaldi changed courses again, quickly surveying the ground below for the flattest stretch of land. As the plane began to descend, he shot Sandhoff a quick glance. "I hope there's some flannel undies stashed away back there, 'cause my guess is we're in for a cold night."

WATCHING HIS BLOOD soak into the surrounding snow, Deton Smith became afraid that he was going to die in this vast white tomb, alone, thousands of miles from home, with a lifetime of dreams and aspirations left unfulfilled.

"Hhh," he groaned, trying to mouth the word "help."

It was thirty degrees below zero along the banks of Young River. Already Smith could feel his hands and fingers going numb from the cold as blood retreated from his extremities. Some of it continued to seep through the exit wound just below the right arm of his bright orange parka. He wasn't sure where the bullet had entered, but somewhere along the way it must have ripped through his spine, because he found himself almost totally paralyzed, aware of slight feeling in his arms and legs, yet unable to move them. And with that paralysis, he realized, so went his chances for survival. Immobile, he couldn't burrow his way deeper into the snow to create a pocket where his body warmth might keep him alive a few hours longer. He couldn't even reach out for the radio walkie-talkie lying half-buried in the snow a few feet away. He tried again to call out, on the chance that he was still broadcasting to the men in the plane. The paralysis had laid claim to his vocal cords as well, however, turning any attempt at speech into a strained, barely audible wheeze, not much louder than the sound of the wind whipping across the tundra.

All Smith could do was lie still, watch himself bleed and try to make peace with his fate.

Through the sifting white powder Smith could see the hulking outline of his sled, piled high with technical equipment and provisions that could sustain any able-bodied man in a position to make use of them. And beyond the sled, though he couldn't see them, the dogs were apparently resting, nine fidgeting huskies unsure of their next move. Now and then he could hear them whine or yelp. If only they were his own dogs instead of a borrowed team. His own dogs would have sensed something was wrong. Somehow they would have made their way to his side and shielded him with their furry warmth. As it was, he could only cling to the faint hope that because it was so close to feeding time they would soon seek him out. Then, if he could somehow communicate with them . . .

But as the elements continued to assert themselves, hope faded and despair began to vie with a growing sense of resignation. Smith's jaw began to tremble, as much from an urge to weep as from the cold. He didn't want to die, and kept repeating the mantra over and over.

As if in answer to his prayer, Smith became aware of a drone in the distance. Squinting through his goggles, he scanned the horizon, rallying at the sight of a plane. It looked small enough to be the Nomad.

Yes! They'd found him! They were coming for him!

Suddenly he heard a series of short, echoing cracks similar to the sound he'd heard when he'd been shot. From the way he was lying in the snow it was difficult for him to place the sounds, but they seemed to be coming from off to his left, near the river.

Up in the sky, the Nomad suddenly changed course, veering away from Smith. He could detect a change in the sound of the plane's engines, too, as they cut back in power. He tried to crane his neck to follow the craft's flight, but it flew beyond his field of vision and the droning faded.

Moments later Smith heard a higher-pitched whine than that of the turbines. As the sound drew closer, he realized it was at ground level and knew it had to be a snowmobile. He also knew that it had to be the gunman who'd fired at him and the plane. He struggled to will his body into motion, but his body paid him no heed. He lay helpless as the vehicle drew closer and came to a stop on the far side of the dogsled.

The engine idled, and Smith could hear someone climb out of the snowmobile and approach his sled. A man in an off-white insulated suit, almost blending in with the cloud of loose snow billowing around him, leaned over the sled, hurriedly sorting through its contents and transferring some of them to the snowmobile. Then, in a harsh, gruff voice, the man shouted at the dogs as he cracked a whip.

"Mush! Mush!"

The dogs stirred and fell into formation as they lurched forward, tugging the unmanned sled behind them. The man stayed put, continuing to yell and crack the whip until the dogs were loping in unison, disappearing into the distance.

Smith next heard footsteps in the thick snow as his assailant grew closer. A fur-lined hood obscured most of the man's head, and his face was half-hidden behind large tinted goggles. Cradled in his hands was a Marlin hunting rifle with a high-powered scope. He leaned over Smith, eyeing the wound left by the rifle.

"Get up."

When Smith failed to respond, the man casually pointed his rifle at his face.

"I said get up!"

The only motion Deton Smith had was in his face. He closed his eyes and pressed his lips closed, as well. It had been more than twenty-five years since he'd recited a certain prayer from his Catholic boyhood, but as he lay there awaiting the inevitable crack of gunfire that would spell his doom, the words came back to him.

Now I lay me down to sleep
And pray the Lord my soul to keep.
And if I die before I wake...

11

Crash landings were nothing new to either Jack Grimaldi or Mack Bolan. Both men had experienced the hellish sensation of being trapped in wounded aircraft, from dead-rotor Hueys in Nam to bullet-riddled Cessnas in the Middle East or wing-shorn Beechcraft Bonanzas in the jungles of South America. In fact, compared to those previous aerial brushes with death, trying to set down a GAF Nomad suffering from little more than a couple of bullet holes and a drained fuel tank was a breeze. After all, Grimaldi had the Nomad under control, and even if the fuel line was to leak dry while they were still airborne, he felt confident he could glide the plane to a landing.

Landing. That was going to be the hard part.

The flurries being swept up by the midday winds hampered visibility as the plane swooped low toward the ground, and there was little way of judging what lay beneath the ever-shifting cover of snow.

"I don't trust the terrain," Grimaldi said. "My guess is the snow's covering a lot of rocks and boulders that'll chew us up."

"That leaves the river," Bolan suggested.

"Yep," Grimaldi said, "and we're going to have a hell of a time making sure we don't come in too close to the embankments."

"I'm sure you can handle it, Jack."

Grimaldi grinned at his long-time colleague. "Famous last words."

"Shut up and drive," Bolan snapped back with mock anger, trying to keep up their morale. He glanced over his shoulder and called out, "You ready for touchdown, Mookie?"

"Working on it," the older man said, desperately trying to strap down the crate he'd been sitting on.

"Kind of wish you hadn't given up your desk job, I bet, eh?" Grimaldi wisecracked.

"Nah," Mookie muttered as he wrestled with an unwieldy clasp. "A little fear now and then's always good for the ticker."

"That's the spirit." Grimaldi stared out the plane's windshield, visibility partially obscured by the onrushing wall of swirling snow. He was barely able to make out the darker outline of the pipeline, much less the snow-swept river. A last-second concern suddenly crossed his mind. "Any chance the river's not frozen over?"

"Deton said it's subfreezing year-round here," Bolan assured him. "It should be plenty thick enough to hold us."

"Well, we're about to find out," Grimaldi announced as they cleared the snow cloud and angled toward the river's silverish gleam. "Hang tight..."

As Grimaldi worked the controls, Bolan crouched forward, tucking his head between his knees and clasping his hands behind his neck. The seat belt would restrain him to a point, but he wanted protection against flying projectiles in the event the landing was as hard as he anticipated. In back Sandhoff positioned himself directly behind Grimaldi's seat and also curled into a ball, bracing himself as best he could.

Had the Nomad been equipped with its customized ski gear, an ice landing would have been far less precarious. But the men had set out with standard wheel gear, and now, as Grimaldi set the plane down on river with a loud, unceremonious thud, the right wheel made contact just before the left, gaining little traction on the slick surface. Almost immediately the plane began to swerve sideways. The ice groaned faintly under the plane's skidding weight but held firm. Grimaldi knew there was little more he could do at this point other than try to keep the right wing from tipping too low and snagging on something that might send the plane cartwheeling.

Upon landing Sandhoff had hurtled forward against the back of Grimaldi's seat, absorbing most of the impact with his right side. He felt something snap just before centrifugal force yanked him backward against the tethered crate behind him. Jolts of pain raced sharply up his side and across his shoulder, almost blacking him out with their intensity.

Bolan, meanwhile, rode out the next few seconds still hunched over in his seat. When the Nomad slowed in the drifting snow and finally slammed to a sudden halt against a steep-rising embankment, he let his body roll with the force of the collision. Only when he was sure the ride was over did Bolan rise from his crouch.

"You okay?" he asked Grimaldi as he unsnarled a headset that had dropped from the ceiling during the landing.

"Yeah." Grimaldi nodded grimly as he turned off the plane's ignition and unclamped his safety harness. "I'm in a hell of a lot better shape than this bird, I'll tell you that much."

Through the windshield both men could see that the Nomad had sustained appreciable damage. The right wing had bent at a sharp angle upon striking the embankment, ripping free of the strut so that the weight of the engine had all but pulled the wing free of the plane's body.

"Looks pretty bad," Bolan commented.

"Nah," Grimaldi scoffed. "Nothing a little masking tape and bailing wire won't fix."

The pilot turned in his seat and glanced back at Sandhoff, who lay on the floorboards just inside the doorway separating the cockpit from the passenger's cabin. "How about you, Mookie?"

Sandhoff grimaced as he sat up, clutching his right side. "I'll live."

"Ribs?" Bolan asked.

"And my hip. Think I dislocated it."

"Sorry," Grimaldi told him.

"Could have been a lot worse. Nice job setting us down."

Grimaldi shrugged. "I've done better."

Bolan quickly sized up the situation and reached behind his seat for a hooded, fur-lined overcoat. "Jack, try to radio for help. I'll go see what kind of shape we're in."

"There's a first-aid kit in back," Sandhoff said, groaning through his pain. "I'll wrap myself up so I won't be deadweight."

Bolan had replaced his lost Desert Eagle with a re-tooled Beretta, and once he'd donned the heavy coat and gloves, he took the gun from his shoulder harness and held it clutched in his palm, realizing that he'd have to pull his gloves off in order to be able to fire it.

"Here," Sandhoff called out as he opened the kit bag and pulled out a pair of safety flares. "You might want to take these."

"I'm not so sure."

"Why not? It'll help us to be spotted, right?"

"Exactly," Bolan said. "By whoever shot us down. If we let them know the crash didn't kill us, we'll find ourselves ambushed."

"Well, we have to let somebody know where we are," Grimaldi interjected as he glanced up from the controls, "and I'm not going to be able to do it by radio."

"What?"

"Afraid so." To demonstrate, Grimaldi turned up the volume on the receiver, failing to pull in static or any kind of signal. He clicked the microphone a few times, too, without anything registering on the output monitors. "I'll try tinkering with it, but I'm sure I'm just going to find cracked circuit boards and loose chips. It's shot."

Bolan traded glances with Grimaldi, then gestured to the FBI agent. "Okay, let me have one flare."

"Here." Sandhoff tossed one of the sticks.

"If this one doesn't bring help, we'll save the other one until we hear a plane in the area."

"Fair enough."

Once he'd pocketed the flare, Bolan eased past Grimaldi and slipped on a pair of snow goggles. Then he leaned his weight into the cockpit door and forced it open.

As he climbed outside, the first stinging blast of cold air quickly alerted Bolan to the harshness of the elements. The subzero temperature was a relatively unfamiliar problem for the warrior. Over the years he'd plied his deadly trade at points all across the globe, but by and large he'd worked in milder climates, and he was far more used to extreme heat than this numbing cold. But for a man like Mack Bolan, the strangeness of this forbidding turf presented a challenge rather than an obstacle. He was determined that there was no way he'd let this be his final resting place.

Although the severest damage had been to the wing, Bolan quickly saw that the overall structural damage to the Nomad was too widespread to hold any hope that it could be repaired, especially under such inclement conditions. With snow already beginning to swirl around the plane's body, he also knew that it wouldn't take long for the Nomad to be buried in a drift, making it virtually undetectable from the air or ground in the event search parties were to begin looking for them. Like it or not, Sandhoff and Grimaldi were right; lighting flares was going to be necessary.

There was minimal tread on Bolan's insulated arctic boots, but with some effort he was able to make his way up the embankment to the mainland. Through the white haze he could see the pipeline, probably a good three hundred yards away. There was no sign of Smith or Miffee, however, not to mention the gunman who'd downed the plane.

Forty yards to the warrior's right was a rock formation rising more than twenty feet into the air. It seemed unlikely that the snow would drift that high, so Bolan hiked over and slowly climbed up to the top. He rearranged a few loose stones, creating a makeshift sconce to set one of the safety flares in. Lighting it was an arduous process in itself, but finally he managed to coax a flame to life long enough to ignite the flare's tip.

Before he descended the rock heap, Bolan stared westward, trying to spot some topographical clue as to the direction of the Eskimo village he'd spotted from the air earlier. He was encouraged at the sight of a small mountain rising a few hundred feet at a point between the river and the pipeline. Thinking back to their aerial surveillance, the warrior recalled the position of the mountain relative to both the pipeline and the village. Unless he was mistaken, if one was to circle around the southernmost base of the mountain and strike a straight course after passing the point where the pipeline crossed the river, he'd be in line to reach the settlement. Of course, once at the mountain, there would also be the option of scaling its peak to get a firmer bearing, since the camp would probably be visible from that altitude once the flurries had subsided. The storm, however, seemed more intent on growing than abating. A sudden, forceful gust of wind whipped up the hill, bowling Bolan off balance. He rolled a few yards downhill before stopping his fall. Crouching, he hugged the rock, waiting for the current to pass. Intensified by the windchill factor, the cold seemed to seep through his clothes, raising knobs of gooseflesh along his arms and legs.

As quickly as it had churned up, the whirlwind dissipated. Bolan slowly made his way down the hill, then headed for the embankment.

When he rejoined the others Grimaldi was helping Mookie bind his lower waist and right thigh with a bandage.

"How's it look out there?" the Stony Man pilot asked as he glanced up at Bolan.

"No red carpet, that's for sure." Bolan went on to explain, concluding, "So it seems like a toss-up whether it's better to head out or stay here and wait for help."

"Well, if it'll help you decide," Sandhoff said, patting his taped side, "like it or not, I think I'm going to have to stay put on the sidelines."

"I checked in back and there's plenty of provisions," Grimaldi said. "Staying put might not be a bad idea."

"Let's play it both ways," Bolan suggested. "Jack, you can stay here with Mookie. I'll bundle up a little more, then strike out on foot. If I don't lose my bearings, it shouldn't take more than a few hours to get to that settlement."

"Don't count on it," Grimaldi said. "That's not sand out there, remember."

"I know." Bolan strapped on a pair of snowshoes and headed out.

12

Deton Smith was still alive. Given his circumstances, however, the wounded man couldn't help wondering if he'd be better off dead.

He was lying inside a cave at the base of Mount Valce, the mountain nearest to where he'd been felled by a single blast of Tom Dinic's Marlin. The Texan was silhouetted in the background, blowing smoke from a cigarette as he paced alongside his snowmobile at the mouth of the cave, talking to someone on a shortwave radio.

It was warmer inside the cave, but only relatively. The perspiration freezing on Smith's face was due to a fever that had beset him over the past hour. His untended wound continued to bleed, his jaw ached from constant trembling, and paralysis left his sizable body in a state of helpless disorder. He could feel his strength ebbing, and along with it not only any sense of hope but also his tenuous grip on his own sanity. There were moments when he was overcome by involuntary fits of strained, hysterical laughter that quickly turned to choked, pathetic sobs.

It was during one such fit that Dinic wandered back into the cave and loomed over Smith, blowing smoke in his face as he shouted, "Shut up!"

When Smith was unable to comply, the Texan lashed out with the back of his mittened hand. Smith's head snapped back, striking the cold rock wall of the cave. He let out a pained gasp and slumped to one side. Dinic reached down and grabbed the collar of Smith's coat, jerking him upright.

"I've had it with you!" he snarled, taking his cigarette and grinding it out on Smith's cheek. "I've had it!"

Smith's mouth gaped open, but he was unable to scream. He felt himself swooning toward unconsciousness and tried to give in to the sensation.

"No, you don't...."

Dinic scooped up a handful of snow and pressed it against Smith's face, shocking him back into consciousness.

"Answer my questions, then you can sleep," the Texan told his prisoner. "Not before!"

Smith stared dumbfoundedly at his tormentor. Answer questions? Wasn't it obvious that he couldn't talk even if he wanted to? Was this man so blinded by his sadism that he couldn't see that? This was too ridiculous, worse than the worst of bad dreams. Ah, now there was a thought. Maybe this was all a dream. Just one of those horrid nightmares that would inevitably run its course, then allow him to wake in a cold sweat, exulting in that first grand rush of realization that none of this had really happened. Yes, a dream. This all has to be a dream. All I have to do is wake up. Wake up, wake up, wake up...

Smith was snapped out of his delirium by the strident whine of a high-compression engine. Dinic cuffed him another time with the back of his hand, then stepped back. Smith's eyes were beginning to swell from the abuse, but he was still able to see out the mouth of the cave.

A second snowmobile slowed to a stop next to Dinic's. Roger Permensen, like Dinic, wore a knee-length hooded parka and huge goggles, making him unrecognizable. He climbed off the snowmobile and exchanged a few words with Dinic as he untethered something strapped to the back of his vehicle. Picking it up, he followed the Texan back into the cave. As they drew closer, Smith was finally able to make out what the stranger was carrying.

"Ever seen a bear trap?" Dinic asked Smith, taking the contraption from Permensen and dangling it by a length of chain. It was spring-loaded, its jaws opened and lined with rows of two-inch teeth. Such traps had been outlawed in most states years earlier because of their unspeakable cruelty to whomever or whatever strayed into their path, but they were still widely used by poachers and indiscriminate hunters. As he swung the trap back and forth in front of Smith's face like a hypnotist trying to entrance a subject, Dinic chuckled. "Why don't we have a look at how it works, hmm?"

The Texan carefully set the trap down, then looked around the cave, coming up with a gnarled tree limb as thick as a man's arm.

"Yes, this will do nicely."

Dinic took the stick and gently prodded a round metal disk lying between the trap's jaws. When he pressed hard enough, there was a loud crack and the jaws clamped shut on the limb with such force that the trap leaped briefly into the air before clattering back to the floor of the cave. Dinic bent over, picking up the stick, which had been nearly severed by the trap.

"See, what they do," Dinic explained, "is sharpen the teeth just enough to bite through fur and flesh but not bone. After all, if it snipped the bear's paw off, it'd still have a chance to get away, right?"

Dinic handed the trap to his associate. With growing horror, Smith watched Permensen strain to pry the steel jaws open. It took considerable effort, and the man had to take care that they didn't snap shut again as he was setting the spring.

"Let's pretend our friend here is a bear," Dinic suggested.

Permensen snorted, and Smith detected a half smile on the man's lips as he crouched over and set the trap flat on the floor between his legs. Even though he was paralyzed, Smith's arms had been tied to his side and his ankles bound together. Once Permensen had the trap in position, he pulled a Bowie knife from a waist sheath and cut the rope around Smith's feet. Dinic crouched and held Smith's right leg firmly against the ground while Permensen raised the other leg and held it out over the open jaws of the bear trap.

"One last time, friend," Dinic whispered to Smith. "Answer my questions. Who are you working with and how much do you know about what we're up to?"

Smith stared at the steel jaws a long moment, then shifted his gaze to the Texan. It required all his concentration to work his tongue enough to fill his mouth with saliva, and it was even more of an effort to purse his lips and fill his cheeks with air. He managed, though, and in what he figured would be his last gesture on earth, he spit in Dinic's face.

"You fucking bastard!" Dinic roared, wiping the spittle from his face. In a fit of fury he dropped Smith's leg and grabbed the trap, handing it to his accomplice. "To hell with his leg! He's not going to talk, so let's snap this thing shut on his neck and be rid of him once and for all!"

BOLAN HAD BEEN OUT for a little over an hour, and he was finally getting used to the snowshoes. They were far more cumbersome than cross-country skis would have been, but he was still covering far more ground than he would have been able to in only his boots. The weather was cooperating more, as the flurries had dwindled considerably since he'd set out. Barring any unforeseen obstacles or delays, he had hopes of reaching the settlement well before nightfall.

As he approached Mount Valce, Bolan broke his stride and slowed to a halt. Half-buried in the drifting snow was a set of snowmobile tracks. Taking a closer look, he also noticed frozen splotches of blood.

The warrior had a decision to make. If it was Deton Smith's blood, it likely had been shed at around the time he'd lost radio contact with the Nomad. Since he'd been reporting from the proximity of the pipeline, it made sense that these tracks were headed in the opposite direction, away from the pipeline and toward the mountain. And since Smith had been traveling by dogsled, it followed that if this was his blood, he'd been taken prisoner, dead or alive. On the chance it was the latter, Bolan quickly resumed his stride, walking alongside the tracks leading to the mountain.

As he drew closer, the Executioner removed his gloves in favor of securing a better grip on his Beretta. He became increasingly concerned when he saw a second set of snowmobile tracks converging with the other near the base of the mountain. Thoughts of the Mertardans came to mind, and he knew it was possible that he'd stumbled onto their hideaway, in which case he could expect to find himself greatly outnumbered.

Pausing behind a large boulder at the base of the mountain, Bolan unstrapped the snowshoes and stepped out of them. He wasn't going to be doing any more overland trekking until he was sure of the situation, and if he found himself drawn into combat, he wanted the increased flexibility he'd have wearing just the boots.

He'd advanced fewer than fifty more yards when he came in sight of the two snowmobiles. Another two steps and he had a clear view inside the cave, where two men were looming over a third, holding what looked to be some sort of hunting trap.

Dropping to a crouch, Bolan took aim at the taller of the two standing men and fired his Beretta.

The slug bored through Permensen's back, just below the shoulder blade. He recoiled from the impact, twisting the bear trap away from Deton Smith's head. The dangling steel jaws teetered in Permensen's hands like an errant pendulum, and when they grazed against his leg the spring snapped. Permensen let out an excruciating cry as the trap clamped down on his thigh, severing an artery. He continued to scream as he fell to the ground, futilely clawing at the blood-soaked trap.

Dinic, meanwhile, shoved Smith aside and dived for cover as a second shot ripped into the cave. Peering out, he couldn't see much because of the blinding white landscape. By the same token, he hoped, he'd probably be equally hard to see as long as he stayed low in the darkness of the cave. Of course, Dinic also knew that as long as he remained in the cave, he was trapped. If there was just one person outside, he could be kept pinned inside until others arrived. If there were others out there, it'd only be a matter of time before they closed in. In either case Dinic knew that one way or another he had to get out of the cave so he could make a run for it.

He considered dragging Smith along as a human shield, but by now he'd come to realize that the man was at least partially paralyzed and as such he'd prove more of a hindrance than help. No, he had to go it alone, and he had to make his move fast.

The Marlin rifle lay propped against the wall a few yards away, but Dinic figured Permensen's two-barreled shotgun would serve him better at this point. Wriggling across the icy ground, Dinic inched past his accomplice, who was still doubled up in writhing agony, unable to pry the trap off his leg.

"Help me, Tom," the wounded man gasped through his sobs. "You gotta help me, man! C'mon, man, I'm begging you!"

Dinic looked away, avoiding Permensen's pleading gaze as he closed his fingers around the shotgun. He was about to crawl away when he changed his mind and backtracked to Permensen's side. Even through the thick clothing, it was clear to see that the man's leg had been nearly severed at the hip by the bear trap, and the blood was still spurting out with gruesome intensity.

"Tough break, Rog," Dinic whispered as he ripped open the other man's parka.

"Wha... What are you doing?"

"Checking your bullet wound," Dinic lied as he quickly frisked the other man. Permensen's chest was bleeding from the exit wound, and when Dinic withdrew a thick envelope from Permensen's shirt pocket, it was drenched red. Blood money.

"You won't be needing this," Dinic told his partner as he slipped the envelope into his own parka.

Permensen gaped at Dinic, a surge of fury bubbling up through his pain. He pulled his hands from the bear trap and tried to grab hold of Dinic, but the man easily crawled away. It seemed likely that Permensen would be dead in a matter of minutes, but Dinic decided not to take any chances he might live long enough to talk to whoever was lying in wait outside.

"See you in hell, Rog," Dinic whispered as he leveled the shotgun at Permensen's face and pulled the trigger. The blast was deafening in the confined space of the cave, and at such close range the explosive force of the charge annihilated Permensen's head even as it was tearing it clear of his body.

The shotgun's thunder was still echoing off the cave walls as Dinic scrambled to a crouch and started for the snowmobiles. Another shot from the outside ravaged the ground at his feet, forcing him to veer to one side and seek the shelter of a squat, half-formed stalagmite. It was then that he realized he was hearing more than just an echo. Most of the noise was coming from outside the cave, and Dinic had spent enough time out in the arctic mountain country to know that the growing thunder could mean only one thing.

Avalanche!

FROM HIS COVER behind the boulders, Bolan had a clear view up the side of Mount Valce, and the avalanche took shape before his eyes. It began when a forty-foot-wide swath of wind-packed snow became dislodged by the echoing blast of the shotgun. As gravity pulled the great white wall downward, it picked up not only more snow, but also loose rocks, debris and eventually even huge boulders the size of tanks.

Bolan was directly in the slide's path, and he knew from the onset that there was no way he could hope to outrun it. Ducking under it was the only feasible chance at survival, and to do that the Executioner had to bolt for cover and charge straight toward the cave.

Halfway to the mouth, Bolan saw Dinic emerging, shotgun clenched in his hands. The other man brought the gun up, but before he could fire, the warrior vaulted over the nearest snowmobile, tackling him. The shotgun, knocked from Dinic's grasp, fell against the side of the snowmobile, discharging wildly with another resonant boom.

The two men wrestled on the ground outside the cave, with Bolan trying to drag Dinic in out of the avalanche's path and Dinic attempting to break free to get to the snowmobile. During the struggle the Texan managed to slam Bolan's right arm against the ground with enough force to send the Beretta flying. By now the first rolling shower of snow and debris was descending upon the valley floor, and when the Executioner felt the sting of stray rock and gravel against his face, he gave in to his instinct for self-preservation. Releasing his grip on Dinic, he rose to a half crouch and sprang backward, hurtling himself blindly through the downpour into the mouth of the cave. His dive took him only a few feet before he slammed into one of the raised stalagmites. His head bore the brunt of the collision and he slumped limply to the ground, knocked out and unable to drag himself clear of the snow heaping itself onto his legs.

Dinic, meanwhile, toppled over the side of his snowmobile and fell to the ground. He started to get up, then quickly ducked back behind the vehicle as the avalanche crushed down on him with all its gathered might. Soon he and both snowmobiles were completely covered.

The slide continued for more than a minute, spreading out as wave after wave of rubble was carried down the slope. By the time it had subsided, tons of fallen snow and debris layered the base of the mountain, in some places drifting nearly twenty-five feet high. There was no trace of the cave. Having taken the worst of the avalanche, the small cavity had been sealed over, burying those inside, dead or alive.

13

From the seventh floor of the Federal Building in downtown Fairbanks, Hal Brognola could see rush-hour traffic clotting the entrance ramp to Seese Expressway. He had no way of knowing that one of those cars heading into the northbound lane contained two of the Mertardan terrorists, both of them carrying falsified passports claiming they were Egyptians in the country on a tourist visa.

"Quite a sight, isn't it?" Michelle Raineswell said as she joined Brognola and shared his view out the window. In the background FBI Special Agent Ralph Schiff was on the phone, having received a call moments before from a field officer back in California.

"I can't quite put my finger on it," Brognola said, "but there's this feeling you get up here. On the surface, Fairbanks looks a lot like any other small town in the lower forty-eight, but then you look a little harder and..."

Michelle smiled. "I think it's the light. Or the lack of it. It takes some getting used to."

"Could be."

"I'll be damned," Schiff muttered, drawing their attention.

"News on the winery?" Brognola guessed.

The agent nodded as he hung up the phone. "As you suspected, Prince Charn was a shadow owner. So no surprise there. But we got a look at their books, and it turns out he was only pocketing a fraction of the profits. Guess where the rest was going?"

"To his uncle?" Brognola suggested.

"Not even close." Schiff picked up a notepad filled with his nearly illegible scrawl. "It turns out all the owners listed on title are also board members for the Eco-Saviors Group."

"Eco-Saviors?" Michelle frowned, confused. "But that doesn't make any sense. They're that radical conservation group, right?"

Schiff nodded. "Yep. They make Earth First and Greenpeace look like Boy Scouts. The thing is, they specialize almost exclusively in opposing oil exploration by the big conglomerates. Off the California coast, down in the Gulf... I think they're even throwing their weight around here in Alaska."

"Ah," Brognola said. "Maybe it's not all that strange after all."

"Not strange for an anti-oil outfit to be backed by the nephew of OPEC's head honcho?" Schiff said. "I beg to differ."

"No, no," Brognola insisted. "Think about it. It makes perfect sense. The Eco-Saviors Group isn't anti-oil in a global sense, or at least I'd bet my prize case of

Havana cigars they aren't. My money says they're solely opposed to U.S. oil exploration and development."

"Which means that the more successful they are, the more we're dependent on foreign oil," Michelle speculated, picking up on Brognola's train of thought.

It fell into place for Schiff, too. "Which means more bucks for OPEC down the line."

"Exactly," Brognola said. "Of course, we've already heard from Sheikh Baibdi's people, and they swear up and down that they had no idea what Prince Charn was up to with his winery."

"Obviously he's lying," Schiff said.

"And obviously he's got something to do with the Mertardans and this whole threat to the pipeline," Brognola added, shaking his head. "Who knows, maybe he's got some of these ecology folks handling this whole operation for him."

"Well, if that's the case, we'll find out soon enough," Schiff declared. The phone rang on his desk, and before he picked it up, he said, "We've got warrants out for all the board members of Whitson-Drew, and you can bet your sweet Aunt Mary that we're going to be grilling them about the Eco-Saviors Group as well as the winery."

Schiff turned away from the others to answer the phone. Brognola and Michelle looked at each other.

"What do you think, Michelle? How active is the Eco-Saviors Group up here?"

"So-so. But I do know they always have flyers floating around at the union halls and the work camps. If they've managed to infiltrate pipeline personnel, well, that might explain where the Mertardans could be getting inside information."

"I don't like this," Brognola said. "Not one bit."

"Neither do I. I was going to wait until tomorrow to get up to see the people at the Tolnera camp, but maybe I should push up the timetable."

"Christ, no!" Schiff groaned on the phone. "Well, look, get some extra people up there, pronto. I'll call the other agencies and try to get them to go priority on it, too."

As the agent slammed down the receiver, Brognola eyed him with concern. "What is it, Ralph?"

"Trouble on Brooks Range."

"Brooks Range," Michelle gasped. "That's where—"

"Something's happened to Belasko?"

"Apparently," Schiff replied. "We've lost radio contact with the plane he, Grimaldi and Sandhoff were in. Not only that, but Deton Smith and Greg Miffee on the ground, too. It's like they just got swallowed up."

"Well, you're sending out search parties, aren't you?" Michelle wanted to know.

"Yes, of course," the Bureau man said. "But it's been more than five hours since any of them called in with their positions. They're out there like needles in a goddamn haystack. We're talking about thousands, maybe hundreds of thousands of acres of area to search through. They could be practically anywhere."

No one in the room wanted to say it, but all three of them were equally aware of an even bleaker prospect—that the terrorists had already struck and the missing parties were dead.

TOTAL DARKNESS.

Total silence.

As Bolan slowly regained consciousness, he battled not only the throbbing pain in his skull, but also disorientation and the unsettling sensation of being trapped in a void. For a fleeting moment he recalled an experimental session spent in a sense-deprivation tank back at Stony Man Farm, when he and several members of Able Team had been strapped inside lightless tanks of shallow water. Was that where he was now? No, it was too cold, the weight on his legs too heavy. What was more, he was lying facedown, not faceup, and he could feel rocky ground beneath him, not the smoothness of the test chamber.

Then it came to him.

The avalanche.

Bolan tried to move. He found he could raise his head, however painfully, as well as his shoulders and his right arm. The rest of his body was immobile, held in the cold grip of fallen snow and debris. He quickly surmised that a portion of the landslide had drifted into the cave, half covering him.

He quickly recalled the circumstances leading up to the time he'd lost consciousness. He doubted that the man he'd wrestled to the ground had survived, but that left the two men who were deeper in the cave. He didn't want to call out on the chance that the man he'd shot was still alive and possibly armed. However, during the few minutes he took to reorient himself, Bolan heard no sounds of life in the cave save for his own and assumed the other two men had died.

When Bolan tried to wriggle his way free, he only succeeded in bringing more snowy rubble tumbling down on him. He stopped moving and waited for the minislide to subside. Still unable to see, he couldn't judge how much rubble was piled on top of him. At some point it had to be as high as the mouth of the cave, otherwise some amount of light would have been able to seep in. If the cave was sealed, it followed that the flow of oxygen was going to be just as limited as that of light. He could breathe with relative ease now, but he wondered how much time he'd have left.

One way or another, he had to get out of there.

When he tried moving again, he restricted himself to smaller movements so as not to disturb the heap he was buried under. It strained his patience, particularly as the cold worked its way through his clothing. He could feel his legs going numb from the way he was lying and the amount of weight being pressed down on them. But he found that by slowly compacting the layer of snow and debris around him, he could create more space for movement without dislodging any of the upper layers. Even though he was able to reach into one pocket for his glove, Bolan preferred the greater maneuverability of working with his bare hand. Every minute or so he would stop to flex his fingers and blow on them to fight off the cold.

It took nearly ten minutes for him to free his left arm in this manner, and more than twice that long before he was able to press back enough rubble to be able to move his entire upper torso. At one point he came across a wide, flat piece of rock. Using it as a makeshift shovel, he spent long minutes painstakingly carving out space around his legs. He was rewarded for his efforts when, at long last, he found he could pull his feet up without resistance. Then, wriggling like some great worm, he eased his way out of the slide.

Which, of course, only solved part of his dilemma. He was still trapped inside the cave, still without light.

Rising to his feet, Bolan stood awkwardly, reaching out for the wall of the cave to support himself. His legs were wobbly and his head still ached, but he tried to tune out discomforts and focus on survival. He shook himself vigorously and stomped his feet, trying to restore his circulation. Once he felt more stable, he put his gloves back on and moved slowly away from the slide, groping in the dark to feel his way.

He'd gone a few yards when his foot brushed against something on the cave floor that gave off a rattling sound. He bent over, feeling the length of chain connected to the bear trap. Following the links, he came across the trap, still clamped to the unmoving body of Roger Permensen.

Taking off his gloves again, Bolan ran his hands over the dead man's body. Ice had formed on the blood-soaked clothes, making it difficult to judge what was in the man's pockets, but finally Bolan found what he was looking for—a pack of cigarettes and, more importantly, the lighter that went with it.

It took a few flicks, but finally the Executioner coaxed a warm tongue of flame from the lighter and held it out before him. He grimaced at the grisly visage of Permensen's headless body but forced himself to inspect the man closer, looking for some clue as to his nationality. He concluded that the man wasn't Middle Eastern, which seemed to discount his theory that he'd stumbled onto the hideaway of the Mertardans.

Moving away from the corpse, Bolan tracked down Deton Smith. He was nearly as blood caked from his wounds as Permensen, but, miraculously, he still had a pulse.

"Deton," Bolan said softly, leaning closer to the security agent. "Deton, can you hear me?"

There was no response. The warrior decided that all things considered, Smith was probably better off unconscious at this point anyway. He did what he could to stanch the flow of blood from the man's wounds, then took off his parka and draped it over him. Bolan was wearing a turtleneck and wool sweater beneath the coat, and he hoped they'd keep him from freezing.

A search of the rest of the cave gave the Executioner a renewed burst of optimism. A knapsack had been left behind, inside which he found a small pack of provisions—food, a flask of bourbon, a flashlight and a tool kit. Returning to Smith's side, Bolan worked by flashlight, cleansing the man's wounds with some of the liquor. Smith flinched involuntarily from the sting of the alcohol but remained unconscious.

Bolan indulged himself with a few sips of bourbon, taking comfort in the burning sensation as it washed down his throat. He quickly wolfed down a piece of jerky and some cheese, then took the tool kit and flashlight and headed back to where he'd been buried by the slide.

In the light's beam, Bolan saw that the drift sloped back toward the mouth of the cave at a gradual angle, which was a good sign.

There was a small, collapsible shovel in the kit bag. Bolan pried open the blade and assembled the handle, then went to the drift. He waded in until the snow and debris were up to his waist, then began shoveling a crude path as he inched his way toward his unseen destination. He found himself gradually heading up an incline of packed snow to the point where he had to crouch to avoid hitting his head against the stalactites.

When he finally reached a spot where the cave ended, Bolan resorted to tunneling, again at an upward angle. He carved his way through another four feet of loosely packed snow, loose stone and boulders, then let out a sigh of relief when the shovel poked through a final layer and created an opening. It might have been the dark of a midwinter day, but compared to the blackness he'd endured in the cave, the dim light was almost blinding.

He widened the opening enough to climb through, then crawled outside the cave, staring at the massive slide that had nearly claimed his life.

It felt good to be alive.

14

Bolan felt that he was racing against time. There was a chance Deton Smith had already died back in the cave, but on the chance he was still alive, the warrior knew that he had to be treated soon if he was to have any sort of fighting chance at survival.

Night was fast approaching, and although the change in light was negligible, the temperature was slowly dropping. With disciplined steadiness, Bolan warded off the cold by working the small shovel against the mound piled in front of the mouth of the cave. He was taking a calculated risk, because there was a likelihood that he could spend all this time trying to unearth the snowmobiles only to discover that the slide had crushed them beyond repair. If they weren't, however, the Executioner figured he could go back into the cave, drag Smith out, load him aboard and still reach the Eskimo village in far less time than it would have taken if he'd set out on foot, particularly without the snowshoes that had been swallowed by the slide.

As he worked, Bolan kept his ears open for the sound of aircraft, hoping that search parties had been dispatched by now and were making their way, by process of elimination if nothing else, to the area around Young River.

Minutes later his shovel clanged off something metallic. He set the tool aside and used both hands to scrape away the snow and rubble covering the first of the snowmobiles. There were superficial dents on the body and gas tank, but at first look the vehicle seemed to be in working order.

The key was in the ignition. Bolan primed the engine, then slowly turned the key. The engine rolled over several times, then finally caught. With a strained whine, the snowmobile spewed exhaust out of its tail pipes. Snow began to melt on the quickly heating engine. Bolan left it running and grabbed the shovel, feverishly hacking at the remaining wall of debris lying between the vehicle and the open arctic plain.

He didn't bother trying to unearth the second snowmobile, figuring that if they weren't rescued and there was still need for it, he could ride back later with Grimaldi and hopefully a better shovel. It seemed a valid enough plan, except for the fact that it didn't take into account the most unlikely of scenarios....

Tom Dinic was still alive.

DINIC HAD HEARD accounts of field workers caught off guard by sudden snowstorms, and those who had lived to tell the tale had all survived the same way—by curling into a ball, remaining calm and letting the snow cover them. When the avalanche descended upon him, Dinic had applied the same technique, dropping down next to one of the snowmobiles, which managed to deflect most of the heavier debris hauled down by the slide. Once it was over, Dinic had been surprised at how well he'd come through it all. Sure, he was buried in a cramped space, but he was alive, could move a little bit, and as long as he remained dry, his own body heat would be sufficient to keep him warm. He had a pint of cheap cognac in his hip pocket, and when he got his hands on it, he drained the entire flask. Then, as he'd been contemplating his next move, the liquor lulled him and he'd nodded off. It had been more than thirty hours since he'd last slept, so it wasn't all that surprising for him to lapse into a deep slumber, a slumber that lasted until he was awakened by the scraping of Bolan's shovel against the other snowmobile, buried in the snow less than three yards from where Dinic lay.

Careful not to betray himself, Dinic had stayed put on the ground, concealed in the snow, listening as Bolan excavated the other snowmobile. It was only when he heard the vehicle's engine turn over that Dinic dared to move. Reaching out, he gently scraped away at the snow around him, finally breaking open a fist-size hole. He could see the other snowmobile and smell its oily fumes. Bolan's back was turned to the vehicle as he carved out a passageway in the snowbank.

Dinic quietly widened the opening with his hands. Then, once Bolan had moved beyond view on the other side of the idling snowmobile, Dinic cautiously wriggled out of his crawl space. He wished to hell he had a gun on him so he could plug the other man in the back and assure himself of a getaway. As it was, though, he still had to get past his adversary. There was some consolation in the fact that the guy was unarmed as well, save for the small shovel.

Dinic rose to a crouch, raising both hands to the handlebar grips of the snowmobile. As he leaned his weight into the rig, inching it slightly forward, he also opened the throttle. The engine responded with a throaty roar.

Less than ten feet away, Bolan whirled, stunned to see Dinic not only alive, but leaping astride the snowmobile, which was already charging forward, directly at him. There was no time for him to get out of the way.

As the snowmobile bore down on him, Bolan sprang into the air, casting aside the shovel. He managed to get high enough so that the impact didn't throw him under the snowmobile's skis. Grabbing the windshield, the warrior straddled the vehicle's sloped nose, riding it backward so that he and Dinic were facing each other.

Barreling clear of the slide, Dinic jerked the handlebars back and forth, veering his course from side to side as he continued to pick up speed. Bolan bounced and slid on the front hood but refused to relinquish his grip. He swung his feet up, finally gaining a toehold on one of the headlight fixtures.

As the Executioner was shifting his weight to free one hand, Dinic leaned forward and lashed out with his fist. He was off balance, however, and landed an ineffectual punch that glanced harmlessly off Bolan's shoulder. The warrior grabbed hold of Dinic's wrist before he could pull his arm back. The Texan lost control of the snowmobile, and it cut sharply to the right just as it came upon a snowdrift. Upended, the vehicle flipped over, throwing the two men to the ground and nearly crushing them as it cartwheeled across the ground.

Bolan rolled with the momentum of his landing and bounded quickly back on his feet. Dinic was a little slower in recovering and had only risen to his knees when the warrior was on him, whipping his right foot through the white powder with a karate kick that caught the Texan squarely under the jaw. With a pained groan, Dinic plopped backward into the snow. Bolan loomed over him, ready to follow through with another well-placed chop. It wouldn't be necessary, however. Dinic was out cold.

To be on the safe side, Bolan leaned over the man, unzipping his parka enough to pull it halfway down his torso. After pulling Dinic's arms out, he knotted the sleeves together tightly, creating a makeshift straitjacket. Then he untied the other man's boots and used the thick laces to bind Dinic's feet together.

Trodding through the snow, Bolan tracked down the snowmobile. It had taken a severe beating, with one ski sheared off completely and the other turned out at an angle from the body. The windshield was shattered, and oil seeped out from under the hood. With some effort Bolan righted the vehicle. Not surprisingly, when he tried the ignition, the engine failed to respond.

He quickly assessed the situation. He was only about fifty yards from the cave. He figured if one of the snowmobiles had survived the avalanche intact, perhaps the other one had, as well. Undaunted, he dragged Dinic to the disabled vehicle and pinned him under it as a further precaution against possible escape.

Bolan was halfway back to the cave when he heard a drone in the distance. Peering into the midwinter sky, he was finally able to make out the lights of an approaching plane.

"That's even better," he murmured to himself as he retraced his steps back to the snowmobile. The engine was out of commission, true, but the battery was still cranking out power. When Bolan switched on the headlight, a lone beam shot out across the snow. As the plane drew nearer, the warrior stepped out into the light and stared upward, waving his arms.

The plane passed by far to his right, apparently following a course along the opposite side of the pipeline. Bolan was concerned that the headlight beam hadn't contrasted enough with the whiteness of the snow to have drawn attention. He continued to wave his arms, though, not stopping until he was sure that no one in the plane could see him anymore.

"Damn," he cursed, lowering his arms and stepping clear of the headlight beam.

He started back toward the cave a second time. He'd only gone a few yards, however, when he suddenly stopped and glanced over his shoulder.

The plane had banked sharply and was doubling back, this time flying over the opposite side of the pipeline. Bolan returned to his signaling position, waving his arms as the plane drew nearer. This time it swooped lower and tilted its wings. There could be no mistake.

He'd been found.

ISOLATED ON AN EXPANSE of barren arctic land between Brooks Range and Prudhoe Bay, Tolnera was one of the coldest spots on the planet. Some pipeline workers, lured by higher wages, volunteered to brave the bitter cold and relentless snowfall. More often than not, after a few weeks they would put in for transfers back to the relatively warmer climes south of the Arctic Circle. Others refused to even consider working the North Slope, referring to Tolnera as Siberia or "The Gulag," a place where one was assigned if he stepped too far out of line with the union.

There were actually two Tolneras.

The workers' camp was composed of scattered timber bungalows and a "Main Street" lined with more bars than shops, churches and restaurants combined. In many ways it was a modern-day Dodge City, primitive, free spirited, and, but for the constant intervention of union enforcers, lawless, as well. After working long shifts on the nearby pipeline, an endeavor invariably fraught with demanding hardship and rampant inefficiency due to the weather and the toll it took on tools and machinery, even the most rugged of individuals returned to the camp in a state of anxious frustration, eager to blow off steam on whatever vices there were to be found. Gambling, drinking and drug taking were rampant. To a lesser extent so was prostitution. Gunplay wasn't uncommon, but usually men were content to settle their differences with their fists. Brawls erupted over the slightest provocation, and often bystanders joined in the action, not so much because they had a stake in the outcome, but because it was something to do.

Contrasting with this Old West in the Great North was another Tolnera, located less than a quarter mile from the work camp. The Ranton Oil operations center, a futuristic structure of thick glass and insulated steel, looked like a space colony in a big-budget science-fiction movie. Situated atop rows of thick pylons anchored to the surrounding permafrost, the building was centrally heated to the point where warm-weathered trees bloomed in its several atriums.

Although workers could secure passes to use the facility's indoor pool, rec room or gymnasium, the space was basically set aside for executives of Ranton and the other oil companies joined in the operation of the pipeline. There were conference halls and office spaces filled with the usual amalgam of computers, secretarial stations and file cabinets, and people were there around the clock, busily at work tending to pipeline affairs. But there were accommodations for pleasure as well as business. In addition to the afore-mentioned facilities, there were also several high-style restaurants serving everything from fine French cui-sine to Cajun gumbo, a ballroom, tennis and raquet-ball courts, weight-training rooms and one's choice of wet or dry saunas. For those executives spending the night with their spouses or high-price "escorts," there was a twenty-room hotel with suites to rival anything offered to dignitaries at four-star establishments.

Rafael Anpard, Ranton's vice president of opera-tions, was indulging himself in the penthouse suite. For the past hour he'd been rolling between silk sheets with a lithe redhead named Sylvie, procured by spe-cial request from an escort agency in Fairbanks. An-pard had arranged to have the woman flown up, at company expense, and would be sending her back in the morning after treating her to a shopping spree at the center's lavish gallery of boutiques. Ranton Oil, and the American consumer, would ultimately pick up the tab for these expenses, which Anpard routinely logged as "specialist consultations."

Spent from their sex play, the woman dozed peace-fully at Anpard's side. He sat up in bed, trying to re-lax. He refilled his champagne flute with the last of the

Dom Pérignon and sipped it as he stared out the picture window, which treated him to a breathtaking view of the northern lights. He was in little mood for scenic wonders, however.

Ever since being summoned to the strategy meeting in Valdez, Anpard's nerves had been on edge. Understandably the prospect of international terrorists blowing holes in the pipeline was enough to unsettle the most tranquil of executive minds. But for Anpard, there was a dark underside to the crisis. Like it or not, he'd been placed in a no-win situation.

If these terrorists made good on their threat and managed to create environmental havoc on the fragile Alaskan tundra, there'd be hell to pay, not only from Ranton and the other members of the conglomerate and their myriad stockholders, but also from the American public. He knew the outcry would be damning, and one of the first heads to roll when it came time for retribution would be his.

But even if by some miraculous stroke the Mertardans were thwarted, Anpard doubted that it would be before the authorities had conducted a careful inspection of the North Slope stretch of the pipeline. Therein lay Anpard's real concern. After all, he'd been charged with making sure that all repairs and renovations of the line were up to code after the string of scandals surrounding shoddy craftsmanship and the use of inferior materials. Millions of dollars had been poured into the project over the past six years, and thanks largely to falsified reports and bribes of inspecting agents, the public impression was that Ranton had made good on its promise to clean up its act.

In fact, a large portion of those millions of dollars had been siphoned off into Anpard's personal accounts, with only a portion of the demanded upgrades being completed according to specifications. In all other instances the work had been purely cosmetic, possibly capable of passing casual inspection, but not the sort of rigid look that would be taken now that officials were stepping in to prevent the Mertardans from gaining access to any so-called weak link in the pipeline.

The whole North Slope was a weak link, Anpard thought to himself sardonically as he swilled the champagne. And by this time tomorrow, the first inspection reports would be coming in.

Of course, by this time tomorrow, Rafael Anpard planned to be on a jet bound for Rio de Janiero. With him he'd have six million dollars in cash and the numbers of bank accounts in the Cayman Islands with twice that amount. It would be sufficient to live off while he eluded the authorities and established a new identity. A new life.

In the meantime he had to go through the motions for another day, feigning concern and pretending to be a team player with the rest of the crisis task force. He was concerned if he didn't, the whistle would be blown and he'd be caught before he could get his hands on the six million which was tied up in bank accounts that required a thirty-six-hour notice for withdrawals an hour after the meeting in Valdez. That left twenty-four hours.

Twenty-three and a half, actually, he noted as he eyed the clock on the wall.

Anpard sighed and lighted a cigarette, then rose from bed and began pacing the spacious bedroom. He was expecting a call from the head of the Pipeline Workers Union, who was flying up from some business in the southern part of the state. There were certain matters that needed discussing immediately.

Ten minutes later the phone rang. It was the union leader, calling from the lobby of the hotel.

"I'll be right down," Anpard said. "I'll meet you in the bar."

He quickly changed and headed out the door, leaving Sylvie to her sleep. He took an elevator down to the ground floor, then stepped out and crossed the lobby, trying his best to look relaxed and unconcerned. He traded smiles with a porter and talked briefly with the night clerk, then made his way into the bar adjacent to the registration desk. The head of the union was waiting for him in a far corner, sipping a dry martini.

"Thanks for coming on such short notice," Anpard said as he slid into the booth.

"No problem at all," Ehki Daifreize replied. "No problem at all...."

15

"And if they dig deep enough, they're going to find out that a lot of that money wound up in your pockets as well as mine, Ehki." Anpard paused to finish his drink, then leveled his gaze at Daifreize. "Do you understand what I'm saying?"

The Saudi nodded. Of course he understood. As head of the Pipeline Workers Union, it was inevitable that he know about the graft and corruption behind the supposed upgrading of the North Slope line. Hell, he'd been a party to it from day one, helping to falsify work orders and inspection reports, painting the wonderful picture behind which the pipeline had continued to deteriorate. He'd been well compensated for his assistance, taking a healthy cut of the appropriated funds as they were diverted from their intended usage. But it had been only a small taste of the big pie, and after months of pondering he'd struck upon his own master plan, his own private agenda. While playing along with Anpard and a handful of other corrupt officials, Daifreize had also made overtures to his native country, eventually striking up his liaison with

Sheikh Leih Baibdi and Prince Widdar Charn, and agreeing to serve as OPEC's top-ranking mole in the U.S. oil industry.

It was Daifreize who had concocted the plan to have the Mertardans sabotage the pipeline, which he knew from his dealings with Anpard was vulnerable to attack on the North Slope. He'd assured Baibdi that if the bombing was linked to Mertarda rather than Saudi Arabia and other OPEC powers, there'd be less of a scandal when it came time for the U.S. to come groveling to the Middle East for more oil. Of course, there'd be those who would claim that Mertarda was acting on behalf of OPEC, but there'd be the usual disavowals by Baibdi and the oil ministers, and perhaps some joint retaliatory measure would be taken against Mertarda to assure the U.S. that OPEC had its heart in the right place.

But this was all in the future. For now there were more immediate problems to be dealt with. Anpard was panicking, and in his concern for covering his ass he was throwing around threats of taking Daifreize down with him if worse came to worst.

That was unacceptable.

"What do you suggest we do?" Daifreize asked calmly as he tapped out a cigarette. They were almost alone in the bar.

"Point the finger elsewhere," Anpard suggested. "That's what we should do."

Daifreize raised an eyebrow. "Scapegoats?"

"Yes. It's worth a try."

"But who?" Daifreize wondered. "If the evidence all points to you—and some at me—then who can we pass the blame onto?"

"If it comes to that, we can say we were framed," Anpard said. "But if we create the right kind of paper tiger, we can throw the authorities off the scent and they might never wise up to us."

"Paper tiger?" Daifreize frowned. "What do you mean?"

Anpard glanced around the bar to make sure no one was eavesdropping. The nearest people were two men across the room. Otherwise there was only a woman sitting at the bar, watching television with the bartender and waitress. She had her back turned to Daifreize, but he thought he recognized her. He didn't have long to dwell on it, however, because Anpard dropped a sudden bombshell.

"Ehki, do you remember Roger Permensen and Tom Dinic?"

Daifreize tried to conceal his shock at the mention of the men's names. For the first time since Anpard had sat across from him, Daifreize was worried that matters had slipped beyond his control.

"Yes, of course I remember them." Daifreize lighted his cigarette and blew a cloud of smoke across the table. "I bounced them from the union for misconduct."

"Exactly. And I just received word tonight that they were caught prowling around the North Slope line near Young River."

"Caught?"

"Well, Permensen's dead, but Dinic's in custody." Anpard went on to explain how a search plane had tracked down Mike Belasko and the others after their plane had been shot down by a sniper, and how Dinic had been subsequently apprehended and taken to a hospital in Fairbanks, where he was discovered to be carrying two envelopes, each stuffed with fifty thousand dollars.

"That's a lot of money for a two-bit hood like Dinic," Daifreize said.

"Well, from the looks of it, half the money was Permensen's and Dinic killed him for it."

"Still, that doesn't explain how either one came into the money," Daifreize said, trying to get a head on how much Anpard and the authorities knew about Dinic's and Permensen's activities since being booted out of Tolnera.

"I know, I know. Which is exactly my point."

"I don't follow you."

"Supposing we fabricate enough evidence to make it look like before Dinic and Permensen were fired, they were involved in bypassing the upgrade measures for the pipeline. We can put it together in such a way that the authorities will think they're somehow in cahoots with these terrorists, probably for some kind of revenge motive, okay? That would send the cops off trying to track down whoever gave them the money that was found on Dinic."

"And what good does that do us?" Daifreize asked.

"It buys us time. Time to do even more damage control."

"What if this 'paper tiger' turns out to be someone linked with the Mertardans?" Daifreize speculated.

"All the better!" Anpard insisted. "The more time spent chasing terrorists, the less time they're going to have to put a magnifying glass on the pipeline."

"I see."

Daifreize finished his cigarette and slowly snubbed it in the ashtray. It was all he could do to suppress a smile. If only Anpard knew that he was looking at the man who'd paid off Dinic and Permensen, the man who was the link behind the bomb threat. Of course, it was imperative that Anpard never come to such a realization. There was only one way to see to that.

"I like your ideas," the Saudi said. "In fact, if you'll excuse me, I'd like to make a few calls and get the ball rolling. I can probably have some evidence put together and planted at Dinic's or Permensen's apartment by dawn."

"That would be perfect!"

"We'll see," Daifreize said. "In the meantime, though, it'd probably be better if we didn't meet in the open like this anymore."

"Of course. You're right. Absolutely."

"Why don't you go back to your room?" Daifreize suggested. "I'll make my calls, then meet you up there. We'll put our heads together and come up with a plan of action."

"Good idea." Anpard slid out from the booth. "Give me a few minutes, though. I have a guest I need to get rid of."

"Of course. I understand." Daifreize offered a knowing wink as Anpard rose from his seat. "One more thing, Raffi."

"Yes?"

"I'm concerned about these terrorists. What have we done to protect the pipeline? In terms of increased security and surveillance."

"We've doubled the security force and the number of aerial runs," Anpard told him, going on to explain timetables and locations. Daifreize listened carefully, keeping clear in his mind the layout of the pipeline. By the time Anpard had spelled out all the measures being taken, he felt a sense of relief. The Young River section of the pipeline was now out of the question in terms of attack, but there were other sections where even the increased protection wouldn't be sufficient to prevent the Mertardans from slipping in and carrying out their mission.

Anpard excused himself and left the bar. Daifreize quickly finished his drink, then retreated to the back hallway.

As he was dialing a number, the Saudi glanced at the bar, this time seeing the woman he'd noticed earlier from the side. It was Michelle Raineswell. Daifreize had locked horns with her several times in the past, always over the same issue—union hiring practices with regard to Native Alaskans. The last thing he wanted to do was get bogged down in a discussion with her tonight. He quickly turned his back to her and waited for an answer on the other end of the line.

He finally got a night clerk at the Anchorage Bay Hotel and asked to have his call put through to the room of Charles Kingsen. Kingsen was a cover name for Ruiz Kalas, lieutenant of Sheikh Leih Baibdi. Kalas answered on the third ring. Daifreize wasted little time on small talk before getting down to the reason he was calling.

"Ruiz, I need you to go to Fairbanks tonight. We have a problem there that needs to be eliminated."

"Problem?"

"Yes," Daifreize said. "His name is Tom Dinic."

MOST OF THE PEOPLE rescued by the search plane at Young River had needed medical attention and had been consequently airlifted to Fairbanks General Hospital. Bolan and Grimaldi had required the least treatment, Deton Smith by far the most. Mookie Sandhoff was diagnosed as having only a severe bone bruise on his thigh.

Thanks largely to his scuffles with Bolan, Tom Dinic had sustained a broken jaw, dislocated shoulder and several cracked ribs. When it was determined that he should remain hospitalized overnight for observation, he was put in a private room with a guard posted outside the door. When the doctors finally gave their okay for the authorities to question him, Dinic proved less than accommodating.

"I know my rights," he taunted from his bed, speaking with difficulty through the wiring around his jaw. "I want a lawyer."

"Yes," FBI Agent Schiff told Dinic, "you've told us that a dozen times already, and it's being taken care of." With him in the room were Bolan and Hal Brognola.

"Fine. When he gets here, I'll talk to *him*."

"If that's the way you want it."

"You're damn right it is!"

Bolan gestured for Schiff to step aside and let him have a crack at the prisoner.

"You know," Bolan told Dinic, "a lawyer is only going to be able to do so much for you. He's not going to waltz in here with a magic wand and change the fact that you're guilty."

"That's something for a jury to decide, isn't it?" Dinic said with a smirk.

"That's right, and a lawyer isn't going to be able to sway a jury after it's heard from eyewitnesses to the couple dozen charges we're already throwing at you, not to mention the ones that will start piling up the more we look into things."

Dinic looked surprised. "Witnesses?"

"Well, there's me for starters," Bolan said. "You shot down my plane, resisted arrest several times—"

"You never said you were a lawman!" Dinic insisted. "I was just acting in self-defense!"

Bolan pretended he hadn't heard. "And then there's Deton Smith," he went on. "He's the guy you shot and then tried to behead with a bear trap. He's alive. Just barely, but he's alive, and I'm sure by the time your court date comes around, he'll be in a position to testify you robbed Roger Permensen, then blew off his head at point-blank range with a shotgun. That's murder one."

"You're lying," Dinic said. "That guy's not alive. No way. And I didn't shoot anybody."

"Nice try," Bolan said. "But it won't wash. And trust me, Deton's alive."

"You're bluffing," Dinic sneered.

Brognola was standing near the door. On Bolan's cue, he opened it and an orderly wheeled in a patient laid out on a gurney. Deton Smith was pale and gaunt, heavily wrapped in gauze and hooked up to several intravenous drippers. He was still unable to move much of his body, but he was very much alive. He raised his head just enough to establish eye contact with Dinic, then lay back. Brognola nodded to the orderly, who wheeled Smith back of the room.

"Convinced?" Bolan asked the prisoner.

Dinic looked shaken. "I want my lawyer," he repeated, this time a little less haughtily.

"When he gets here, your best bet is going to be to think in terms of cutting a deal," Schiff advised.

The Texan hesitated a moment, then muttered, "What kind of deal?"

"We want to know who hired you and Permensen and what you two were doing out by the pipeline," Schiff said.

Dinic didn't respond.

"Look at it this way," the agent suggested. "I've added it up and the way it stands, once we finish with you in court, you'll be looking at a few hundred years' worth of hard time, and that's providing we can't figure out a way to give you the chair. It's up to you to whittle those years down to some kind of sentence you have a chance of outliving. It's a lot of years. You're going to have to do a lot of talking."

"All right, all right. I'll think about it!" Dinic snapped. "Now get the fuck out of here and leave me alone!"

"Sure thing, Tommy. We'll send your lawyer in as soon as he gets here. But, trust me, he's going to be telling you the same things we're telling you now."

Schiff led Bolan and Brognola out of the room. They walked past the guard standing outside the door and started down the hallway.

"He'll talk," Schiff guessed.

"We better hope so," Bolan said. "I have a feeling we don't have much time left."

"What do you mean?" Schiff asked. "You don't really think they're going to try to go through with anything now that they know we're on to them, do you?"

"Maybe not," Bolan conceded. "But we can't count on it. The stakes are too high."

"I agree." Brognola said.

"How are we coming on our other fronts?" Bolan wanted to know.

Brognola reported that Greg Miffee and the other teams who'd been out exploring the pipeline had been called off during the onset of the snowstorm. If weather permitted, they'd head out again first thing in the morning.

Schiff next brought Bolan up to date on the connections made between Whitson-Drew Vineyards and the Eco-Savior Group, concluding, "A couple of the workers have been talking, and they say the reason the winery was so heavily guarded was because Charn was trying to get the group to go militant. He was planning a raid on one of the oil-company headquarters in San Francisco next month."

"Then it didn't really have anything to do with the Mertardans," Bolan said.

"Who knows?" Brognola surmised. "If things had gone well up here, the Mertardans might have been brought down and thrown in with whoever they were planning to use for the raid."

"What about the guy in the blue sweats?" Bolan asked. "Any identification yet?"

Brognola shook his head. "No, and nothing on the other two men, either. I've got Kurtzman trying to raise McCarter and the rest of the Phoenix Force to see if they recognize the mug from any of their missions in the Middle East, but he hasn't gotten back to me yet."

They reached the end of the hallway. Schiff excused himself and headed outside to his car. Brognola and Bolan ventured into the cafeteria and bought cups of coffee. The Executioner kept running things through his mind, trying to get the pieces of the puzzle to fall into place. Something occurred to him.

"Is Michelle Raineswell having any luck checking through personnel?"

"She's working on it. Once we got word that this Dinic character's mixed up in things, she decided to hightail up to Tolnera to sniff around. That's the last known address we have for either Dinic or Permensen."

"Tolnera." From all he'd been told about the workers' camp, Bolan found it hard to imagine Michelle Raineswell there. She'd be out of her element, he was sure of it. The thought of her getting in over her head with some of the local lowlifes was disturbing. He tried to shake the image from his mind.

It wasn't easy.

16

Impeccably dressed in a navy suit and polished brogues, Ruiz Kalas sat in the lobby at Fairbanks General, feigning interest in a back issue of dog-eared magazines. There were several other people in the area, most of them watching the local news on a television dangling from a ceiling mount. Kalas glanced up when he heard a news anchor launch into a story about the search-and-rescue operation near Young River. Obviously the press had been given a sanitized account of what had happened, as there was no mention of any terrorist threat to the pipeline or the fact that the man found slain in the cave had had his head blown off with a shotgun after a bear trap had chomped away half his thigh. The official slant on the story was that Dinic and Permensen were nothing more than a couple of ex-pipeline employees who'd been caught trespassing along a stretch of the North Slope line, where they had apparently stockpiled some of the drugs they'd been peddling prior to their eviction from the work camp in Tolnera. The story ended with confirmation that Dinic would be arraigned the following afternoon.

That's what they think, Kalas thought to himself. As the news went to commercial, he turned his attention back to the magazine, all the while maintaining his discreet vigil on the information window located just to his right.

Nine minutes later a man wearing a knee-length wool coat over a dark suit entered the hospital, carrying an alligator-skin attaché case. He passed Kalas as he headed directly for the information window.

"I'm here to see one of your patients. Thomas Dinic," the man told the woman behind the window.

"I'm sorry," the woman said after scanning her computer, "but Mr. Dinic isn't allowed visitors."

"I'm his attorney." The man produced a business card and handed it over. "Now, please, what room is he in?"

"He's in 623A," the woman said, returning the man's card.

"Thank you."

As the lawyer headed across the lobby, Kalas rose and fell in step beside him, intercepting him near the elevators.

"I'm sorry, sir," Kalas said in an officious tone, "but I need to search you before you go up."

"I'm his lawyer, for Christ's sake!" the other man protested indignantly.

"Sorry, sir, but those are my orders. It will only take a minute," Kalas insisted, gesturing to the nearby stairwell. "If you could step over here, we don't want to alarm any of the other visitors."

Fuming, the lawyer followed Kalas into the stairwell. "If you don't want to alarm anyone," he grumbled, "you might have at least waited until we were up on the—"

The Saudi cut off the man's last words, clamping his hand across the lawyer's mouth. Kalas had two inches and a good thirty pounds on the lawyer, and when he threw the man off balance and slammed his head into the concrete wall of the stairwell, it was with enough force to crack the man's skull. He dropped limply into Kalas's arms.

The Saudi had cased the area earlier and knew that there was a janitorial storage room around the corner. He dragged the other man into the darkened chamber, dumping him behind some cardboard boxes filled with toilet paper. Then, withdrawing an automatic .22 with a silencer, he took aim at the lawyer's head and pulled the trigger. One shot was sufficient to make sure the man would stay put.

Kalas slipped the gun back into his shoulder holster and left the storage room. He picked up the attaché case where the lawyer had dropped it, then exited the stairwell and strolled casually to the elevators. The doors were closing on one of the cars. Someone inside pressed a button, reopening the doors long enough for the Saudi to step in.

"Thank you," he said.

"Which floor?"

"Six."

RAFAEL ANPARD HANDED Sylvie five hundred-dollar bills.

"Here, sweetheart, these will keep you company."

She took the money and smiled as she slipped them inside the waistband of her panty hose. She was half-dressed, sitting on the edge of the bed as she slipped her petite feet into a pair of velour pumps.

"How long do you want me away?" she asked.

"Not long. An hour, hour and a half at most." Anpard motioned for her to stand. He was holding her blouse, and as she slipped her arms through the sleeves, he leaned close and kissed the back of her neck. "When you get back we'll pick up where we left off."

"Mmm, I can hardly wait." Sylvie let her hand trail down to Anpard's groin. She squeezed him slightly, then moved away, humming contentedly as she stepped into her black leather minidress.

Anpard walked with her to the door, then drew her into his arms for another embrace. "I'll miss you."

"Good." Sylvie kissed him, then pulled away. "Oh, by the way, I ordered up more champagne, but don't pop the cork until I'm here."

Anpard chuckled. "Believe me, the way you pop my cork, you can count on it."

They shared another laugh as Anpard unlocked the door and reached for the doorknob. It was already turning, however, and before he had a chance to re-act, the door suddenly flung inward, slamming into Sylvie. She let out an involuntary cry as Ehki Daifreize stormed into the room, a switchblade clutched in his gloved hand. Wasting neither time nor motion, the Saudi strode directly up to Anpard and plunged the six-inch blade deep into his chest. As he twisted the knife, he moved in close to the oil executive until they were eyeball to eyeball.

"I think you'll make a better scapegoat," Daifreize whispered.

Blood bubbled up through Anpard's lips and life faded from his gaze as the Saudi let go of him, letting him fold to the carpet, staining it with his blood.

He next turned on Sylvie, who was staring with slack-jawed horror at the body of her fallen lover. As Daifreize closed in on her, she opened her mouth to scream. He strangled her cries, though, clamping his fingers around her throat as he leaned into her, shoving her against the wall. She struggled in his grip, but was no match for his superior strength.

"A jealous lover," he told her calmly as he watched her face turn color. "Maybe he jilted you, maybe you jilted him. It doesn't matter. The police know about these crimes of passion...."

Sylvie managed to kick Daifreize in the shin, but he refused to relinquish his grip until he'd choked the life from her. Then he let her fall into his arms and dragged her next to Anpard's body. He laid her out on her back and transferred the bloodstained switchblade to her hand, then shifted Anpard's body as well, positioning his hands around the woman's neck, which was clearly marked with dark welts where Daifreize had strangled her.

Standing over his victims, the Saudi briefly admired his handiwork. Anpard was no longer in a position to make threats, much less carry them out. All that remained now was for Daifreize to assemble the Mertardans and assault the pipeline. If the job was done right, the line would be damaged beyond the point where anyone should bother worrying whether there'd been inadequate repairs. If they did, the evidence would point to Anpard's complicity, not Daifreize's.

He spent a few minutes searching the penthouse, making sure there was no evidence that would draw attention his way once the police were summoned to the scene. Satisfied he was in the clear, he let himself out of the apartment, pausing outside the door long enough to flip the placard hanging on the doorknob so that it read Do Not Disturb.

"DID THE FOOD do anything for that headache?" Brognola asked Bolan as they emerged from the cafeteria.

"Not really. But I doubt it'll be fatal."

Brognola checked his watch, then glanced up and down the hallway. "Still no sign of Schiff." The FBI agent had agreed to rendezvous with Bolan and Brognola in the cafeteria more than ten minutes earlier but hadn't shown up. "I wonder what's keeping him."

"Beats me. Maybe we got our signals crossed."

"Not likely."

Brognola led the way to Dinic's room, asking the guard stationed outside the hall, "Has Agent Schiff been back here since we left?"

"No, sir," the guard said. "Dinic's lawyer got here about five minutes ago, but that's been it."

"Ah, the lawyer. Let me just find out how much time he thinks he's going to need."

Brognola knocked on the door. When he received no answer, he knocked again. "Excuse me," he said, opening the door and sticking his head in, "but I was just... Hello?"

As the big Fed's voice trailed off, Bolan asked him, "What is it?"

"He's not in here."

"Dinic?"

"No, the lawyer."

Brognola and Bolan entered the room. Dinic was still in bed, apparently asleep. There was no sign of the lawyer other than his attaché case, which lay open at the foot of the bed. Brognola heard the sound of running water and directed his attention to the washroom in the corner of the room. The door was closed, but a shaft of light was visible underneath it.

"Excuse me," Brognola repeated, moving toward the door. "My name's Brognola and I'm with the Justice Department. If you could just let us now how long you'll need with your client, we'll—"

"Don't waste your breath," Bolan called from Dinic's bedside. "I don't think there's anyone in there."

"What?"

Brognola turned and saw Bolan withdrawing his Beretta from its holster as he moved from the bed to the nearby window.

"Dinic's dead. Some kind of injection."

Brognola spotted a hypodermic needle lying on the bed next to Dinic, along with a small glass vial.

"He had to have gone out this way," Bolan said, jerking the window open. "Call security and get them to seal off the grounds!"

A cold blast of air greeted the warrior as he crawled onto a narrow ledge running beneath the window. There was a fire escape several windows away, and he traced the sound of footsteps clanging on metal until he spotted a man already four floors down, bounding down the steps two and three at a time.

The Executioner inched along the ledge until he reached the fire escape, then climbed onto the landing and took aim over the railing. He fired at the fleeing murderer, but there was too much metalwork in the way for him to hit his mark.

Alerted by the gunshots, Kalas stopped on the second-floor landing and returned fire, smashing a window just to Bolan's right. Rather than waste his time firing back, the warrior took up the chase, scrambling down the zigzagged staircase. In his haste he nearly slipped on built-up layers of ice several times, but it was worth the gamble as he closed the distance between himself and his quarry, who was delayed briefly when he had to unfasten a latch in order to drop the final length of stairway to ground level.

By the time Kalas cleared the fire escape and began running across the asphalt of the parking lot, there was no sign of hospital security, and the Executioner was still two stories up. But Bolan hadn't come this close only to let his man get away. Climbing onto the railing, he bent to a crouch, then sprang into the air. He wasn't foolish enough to think he could nail his quarry with a flying tackle. Instead he directed his fall toward a trash Dumpster filled to overflowing with garbage from the cafeteria. As he'd hoped, most of the refuse consisted of paper goods stuffed into plastic bags, which formed an adequate cushion for him to land on. And because the Dumpster was over-filled, the warrior was able to tumble quickly to the ground. He somersaulted partially and was back on his feet.

Kalas had heard Bolan's fall, and he fired at the Executioner, clanging hot lead off the Dumpster before resuming his flight. Weaving madly through a clot of parked cars, the Saudi reached a chest-high fence and stuffed his gun inside his waistband so he could use both hands to clear the barrier.

Bolan hurdled a few pylons trying to gain ground and reached the fence seconds after his quarry. He vaulted over easily and hit the ground running.

They were less than half a block from one of the busier sections of downtown Fairbanks. Bolan didn't want the chase to extend into pedestrian traffic. At the risk of losing ground he'd just gained, he quit running and planted himself, drawing aim at the fleeing figure.

"Freeze!"

When the man kept running, Bolan blasted away with a 3-shot burst. Two slugs skimmed off the pavement near the killer's feet, but the third hacked into the back side of his thigh. Thrown immediately off stride, the man veered to his left, slamming into the side of a brick-walled office building. He grunted with pain and quickly pushed off, pulling out his gun. It only took him a couple of steps to realize the extent of his wound and know he was no longer capable of running.

"Put the gun down," Bolan demanded.

Kalas looked defeated. He held his hands out to his sides and seemed about to drop the gun when he suddenly brought it up into firing position. Bolan, however, wasn't taken by surprise. He got off three more shots in the time it took Kalas to fire one. Three 9 mm parabellum slugs pounded into the Saudi's chest, knocking him backward as his own shot drilled harmlessly into the asphalt near his feet.

Bolan slowly advanced and stood over his quarry. The man was already dead. He'd silenced Dinic and had been subsequently silenced himself. It made sense that the dead man fit somewhere into the puzzle, probably somewhere between Dinic and whoever was masterminding this whole sordid episode. But overall Bolan felt he was no closer to intercepting the Mertardans than he had been when the bloodshed had begun in Cinnaton.

There was commotion in the background and several hospital security guards rushed out of the main gate, heading for Bolan with their guns drawn.

"You're a little late," he told them. He was beginning to feel there would be those who would be saying the same thing to him, only they would be talking in terms of his failure to thwart the Mertardans from achieving their nefarious objective.

It was time to screw official procedures and go with his gut. When Brognola showed up with the security forces, Bolan took him aside.

"Let's get our butts to Tolnera," he said determinedly. "Now."

17

The Yukon Rush was one of the most popular bars on the main drag in Tolnera, and Ehki Daifreize made a point of making his presence known during the hour he spent there after leaving the Ranton operations center. He caroused with the workers, bandying about his share of bawdy limericks, lost a few dollars at the pool tables, made a few supposedly drunken passes at the waitresses—all ploys to leave an impression on people's minds on the remote chance he might need an alibi for his whereabouts at the supposed time of the penthouse killings of Rafael Anpard and his companion. If it came to that, of course, he had some loyal followers who would swear he'd been at the Yukon a couple hours earlier, but it'd be better if there were others who recalled him being there during roughly the same time frame.

Amid all the revelry there was also an undercurrent of talk, regarding the fate of ex-workers Roger Permensen and Tom Dinic. The news had just come in about Dinic's mysterious death at the hospital in Fairbanks, and there were those who saw the two men as working-class martyrs whose deaths could be laid to some clandestine conspiracy being perpetrated by Ranton Oil executives. As rumor had it, Dinic and Permensen were out at Young River gathering evidence that the corporation had skimmed funds earmarked for pipeline upgrades and had subsequently substituted cheaper, inferior materials for the repair work. After all, most of the work in question had been done by union laborers from the Tolnera camp, and there had been countless incidents where questions about quality of materials had been raised at the work site, only to be shrugged off by supervisors who, if pressed, would promise to have the matter looked into. Invariably, whenever such questions arose, the work crews would be transferred to another site miles away before getting the chance to see if anything was actually done.

As head of the union, Daifreize felt an obligation to side with the workers, but their suspicions were so close to the truth that he found himself trying to shoot holes in their arguments or change the subject to other matters, particularly a major wage-increase package he was currently in the midst of negotiating with Ranton management.

When he finally did leave the bar, it was with relief. All the gossip had gotten on his nerves, which were already frayed from the long string of misadventures that had begun with his slaying of Stasha Darvin back in California. It seemed as though his master plan was falling apart on him, and indeed he'd been putting out one fire after another, with another always cropping up. And yet the bottom line was that despite all the snafu, the mission was still intact. The Mertardans had all been successfully smuggled into the country and were gathered in Tolnera, awaiting orders. The explosives had been secured, as well—a deadly combination of plastique, dynamite, grenades and even a few Stinger missiles. And, at least for the time being, the pipeline remained vulnerable enough in certain key spots to be irreparably damaged.

The weather was playing into his hands, too. This afternoon's storm had warded off the search teams that might have otherwise discovered the extent of shoddy repair work done on the North Slope over the past few years. That had bought him more time, and as he looked to the north, he could see another front rolling in from off Beaufort Sea. Forecasters were saying it would be as widespread and furious as the last one, which meant that aerial surveillance flights would be disrupted and the added security forces would be seriously hampered from carrying out a thorough inspection of the pipeline. Such conditions would provide an ideal cover for the Mertardans to steal in and do their job.

As he strode across the snowbound street, Daifreize saw a lone police car out on the service road linking the work camp with the operations center. Its roof lights were on and it was speeding toward the center, where another three squad cars were visible, along with a paramedic's van.

The bodies had been found, Daifreize surmised. If police were still arriving, that meant the discovery had to have been just a few minutes ago. That was a good sign. Provided the coroner couldn't pinpoint an exact time of death, Daifreize felt he now had more than sufficient leeway in terms of his alibi.

He strolled past a few more bars and restaurants, then turned down a side alley leading to the workers' bungalows. There were twelve of the two-story structures in all, each designed to house up to a dozen men. During the boom years of the pipeline's initial construction phase, all twelve of the bungalows had been constantly in use, at times at twice their capacity. That had been fifteen years ago. Now it was a rarity when seven of the buildings were in use as living quarters for the maintenance and repair crews. Those bungalows located farthest from the main road had been converted to warehouses.

Daifreize made his way to one of the back buildings separated from the others by an icy knoll. Some supplies were stored there, but its primary function these days was as a gathering hall for union meetings, the next one on schedule for the following Wednesday. Until then, there was little reason for anyone to bother making the trek out to the building, especially since the walkway had been drifted over by the afternoon storm. The lone tracks leading to the building had been made by a supply truck that had arrived earlier that evening, supposedly with a load of high-tech welding gear slated for use next spring when the pipeline's joints were due for their annual inspection. Two of Daifreize's most loyal lieutenants had manned the truck, however, and they'd been carrying a far different cargo—the eight-man Mertardan bomb squad.

As he approached the bungalow, Daifreize took out a penlight and flashed a coded signal at one of the front windows. A moment later a return signal was given, and by the time he reached the side door, the dead bolt had been thrown open. Daifreize was let inside by his right-hand man, Andres Gottseed, a veteran wildcatter hailing from Corpus Christi, Texas. It was Gottseed who'd first shown Daifreize the ropes of the oil business and given him his taste for Western wear.

"Hey, hey, Ehkster," Gottseed drawled, giving his long-time friend a hearty slap on the back as he stepped out of the cold. "With all this shit hitting the fan I was beginning to wonder if I was going to see you again."

"You know me, Andy," Ehki told the other man. "I'm a survivor."

"Ain't that the truth."

"How about you?" Daifreize asked. "Did everything go well on your end?"

Gottseed nodded. "Yep. C'mon, you can see for yourself."

The Texan led Daifreize through the vestibule and into the meeting hall. There was only a single light burning in the corner, giving the chamber a ghostly appearance. Rows of empty chairs were lined up before a podium, and off to one side was a card table filled with union literature.

As the men crossed the room, Gottseed muttered, "Tough break with Kalas, huh?"

"Kalas?" Daifreize repeated, taken aback. "What do you mean?"

"Oh, I assumed you'd heard," Gottseed said. "He got iced down in Fairbanks, apparently right after he'd taken out Tom Dinic."

Daifreize couldn't believe it. Kalas dead? That had to be the worst of all the omens he'd had to contend with the past couple days. He refrained from showing Gottseed any sign of undue concern, however.

"Price you pay."

"Listen, I also heard about Raiko and Atmon," Gottseed said as they passed through a second archway and started up a staircase leading to the upper floor. "Sorry..."

"I loved them, but they both got what they deserved. I'm just glad it wasn't left to me to take care of them."

Halfway down the hallway, Gottseed stopped and opened a door, gesturing Daifreize into one of the upstairs rooms.

The windows were covered with plywood so no one outside could tell there were lights on. Inside the room, gathered around a humming space heater, were the eight Mertardans. At first glance there was little about their appearance or demeanor to suggest that they could be capable of posing any kind of threat. All of them were shivering, still unused to the dramatic change in temperature from their homeland. Some were nursing cups of coffee, others tea or small bowls of soup.

Daifreize wasn't put off by the men's apparent frailty. He knew of their reputation, their indisputable professionalism in the world of terrorism and sabotage. And if there had been any doubts, they would have been dismissed upon taking a good look into the terrorists' eyes.

To a man, the Mertardans had the looks of the truest desperadoes—those already dead inside. These were men whose lives had been given over to a cause, men without families who had nothing to lose and were therefore unlikely to have their missions compromised by timidity or excessive concern for self-preservation. Sure, if they could survive from mission to mission, they considered it a good thing, but only in the sense that it left them in a position to put their lives on the line again in the pursuit of their cause.

Their cause this time around, of course, was furthering the political gains of their country by aiding in the destruction of the pipeline.

As a courtesy, Daifreize greeted the men in their native language, thanking them for their commitment and for putting up with the inconveniences surrounding their various forms of entry into the States.

Once he had their attention, the Saudi launched into the business at hand.

"Listen to me very carefully," he told them, "because we have time for me to go over our plan only once. When I'm finished, we'll leave and set out for our target areas.

"We strike at dawn."

GRIMALDI AND BOLAN had just gotten word of the penthouse killings while en route to Tolnera, so they were prepared when they spotted the cluster of police cars outside the Ranton Oil operations center. They were in a small Bell chopper, and as Grimaldi guided the aircraft to a landing on the heliport set atop the roof of the oil complex, he said, "Death really seems to be in season up here."

Bolan didn't respond. As soon as the Stony Man pilot killed the engines, he unstrapped himself from his safety harness and disembarked. Thermal lines running under the heliport's landing pad kept it from icing over, and the men's footsteps were muffled as they padded toward the receiving station. A security officer was waiting for them in the doorway. After a glance at their IDs he let them inside, where they took a flight of steps leading down to the penthouse.

As they cleared the last of the steps, Grimaldi ventured, "Seems a little odd that with all this cloak-and-dagger stuff going on Anpard would wind up dead from something that has nothing to do with anything else."

"Yeah, it crossed my mind, too."

They had to show their credentials a second time to gain entry to the penthouse. The coroner had just arrived, so the bodies were still sprawled across the carpet where they'd been found by a room-service porter bringing up the fresh bottle to the suite. Plainclothes homicide detectives were combing the room for clues while a pair of uniformed officers kept vigil near the door, keeping curiosity seekers from getting in the way.

"So, how do you figure it?" Grimaldi asked Bolan once they'd surveyed the scene. "Maybe she was more than just a high-price hooker."

"I don't know," the warrior replied. "If somebody wanted Anpard knocked off, they would have used a pro."

"True."

"Of course, maybe that's what happened." Bolan turned to one of the homicide dicks. "The bodies haven't been moved yet, right?"

"Well, not by us," the detective told him.

"But they were moved by someone," Bolan guessed.

The detective nodded. "Yeah, I'd say that's a pretty safe bet."

"How do you figure?" Grimaldi asked.

Bolan pointed at the bodies. "That blood on the carpet behind Anpard. See the way it's smeared? Like he was killed a few feet away, then dragged over next to the lady."

Grimaldi nodded.

The detective eyed Bolan with grudging admiration. "Nice call, Sherlock. There's a few other things that don't add up, either. Anpard's hands don't match up with the bruises on the lady's neck, and then there's the fact the switchblade's too big for her purse. She's not wearing anything she could have had it concealed in, either."

"Maybe it was Anpard's," Grimaldi suggested.

"Maybe, but I doubt it. Only prints on it are hers, and it looks like it was wiped clean before it wound up in her hands. My vote says it's a plant."

"Any suspects?" Bolan asked.

"Nothing solid, but there's one guy we're trying to track down for questioning," the detective said. "Ehki Daifreize. Heads up the workers' union here. A real big shot. Practically runs the work camp. Anyway, the switchboard operator says he put a call in to Anpard earlier this evening and the folks in the bar downstairs say the two of them met there a few hours ago."

Daifreize's name didn't register with Bolan, but he was concerned by the description of the man's clout and duties. If there was indeed a mole in Ranton passing along details on pipeline operations, the head of the workers' union seemed as likely a suspect as anyone.

"You said you're trying to track him down?" Bolan asked the detective.

The man nodded. "We've tried paging him here at the center. Zip. They tell me he's not big on wearing a beeper, so it's not like we can reach him with a quick call if he's over at the camp."

Bolan thanked the detective for his help and led Grimaldi out of the penthouse. As they headed for the elevators, the pilot saw the concern on Bolan's face.

"What's up?"

The Executioner waited until they were in the elevator and on their way down. "If he heads up the union and Michelle Raineswell came up here to check on personnel for possible moles . . ."

"Whoa, buddy, whoa. Don't get ahead of yourself. I'm sure she's fine."

Bolan hoped Grimaldi was right, but his gut was making another call. The woman was in possible danger. He could feel it. He just hoped he'd be in a position to do something about it.

MICHELLE RAINESWELL had a number of trusted, well-placed contacts with both pipeline labor and management in Tolnera. After arriving at the isolated town, she'd dutifully contacted as many of them as she could, either by phone or in person. She began at the operations center, speaking to a diverse group ranging from a vice president of special services to the waitress and bartender at the ground-floor cocktail lounge. Once she'd finished there she'd taken the shuttle to the work camp, where she'd mingled with some acquaintances at a few bars and restaurants. Not being able to mention the threat of terrorist sabotage, it was difficult for her to fish for the kind of information she wanted, but she tried her best. She asked questions intended to provoke responses that might have given away anyone aware of the Mertardan situation, and inquired about any suspicious activity taking place at the work camp or operations center. The latter tactic earned her an earful of shoptalk and gossip about the usual array of office politics—people having affairs, people stealing office supplies and clothing rations, people threatening to quit their jobs. The bottom line, however, was that after seven hours of almost nonstop "investigation," Michelle felt she was no closer to unearthing a link to the terrorists than she had when she'd left the strategy meeting in Valdez.

Not that she was surprised. After all, she'd never claimed to be a spy catcher, and she found the whole cloak-and-dagger enterprise a deplorable necessity she was ill suited for.

It was late and Michelle was more than ready to call it a night. First, though, she decided to stop by the Native Council's Tolnera walk-in center, one of the converted back-alley bungalows off Main Street. The center was open twenty-four hours a day, providing low-cost medical care and counseling, overnight lodging for workers who'd come up short on cash between paychecks, and a recreation room where one could spend time without feeling the temptation to squander wages at other establishments in town.

Most of the workers and employees knew Michelle by name and exchanged greetings as she toured the facility. She'd helped start this center as well as eight others like it located along the pipeline corridor, and it made her feel good to go in and see the place filled with fellow Aleuts and other Natives making the best of their lives. Her joy, however, was tempered by the thought of what might happen to these people should the pipeline be rendered inoperable for an extended period. Jobs were hard enough to come by in Alaska; if there were massive layoffs at Ranton, most of the Native work force would be among the first to be let go. Sure, it was unfair, but Michelle knew the political makeup of the state as well as the oil companies, and when push came to shove, she knew it would always be her people who would come out on the short end of the stick.

It was while she was visiting with a few of the workers that Michelle first heard about the penthouse killings. She couldn't believe it at first. Why, just this morning she'd been arguing face-to-face with Anpard, and a couple hours ago she'd seen him talking with someone in the cocktail lounge at the operations center. And now he was dead. Murdered. It didn't seem possible.

Or did it?

Michelle suddenly recalled that Anpard had supposedly been engaged in the same task she was, ferreting out the mole supplying the Mertardan terrorists with vital statistics on the pipeline. In light of that, his death took on a new and ominous significance.

Excusing herself, Michelle left the rec room and headed up to the main office on the upper floor, exchanging a few pleasantries with the secretary on duty before asking to borrow the phone.

"I can't believe you think you have to ask!" the secretary said as she rose from her chair. "Please, help yourself. I have to run a quick errand anyway, so you can have some privacy."

"Thank you."

Michelle waited until she was alone to dial the phone. Bureau Agent Schiff had given her a number where he could be reached in Fairbanks. She was relieved when he answered. Quickly she explained how she'd spent what she at first thought was a futile, unproductive day. "But now I'm worried," she went on. "I know what they're saying about Anpard being killed by some mistress or something, but what if there's more to it than that? What if he inadvertently warned the mole we were looking for him?"

"We're looking into that possibility," Schiff told her. "And to be safe, you'd be wise to steer clear of anybody you've dealt with today, too."

"Yes, of course," Michelle said, feeling a knot form in the pit of her stomach. Schiff was confirming her worst fear—that perhaps the person who killed Anpard was someone she'd questioned earlier, in which case she might find herself the next target.

"Where are you right now?" Schiff asked.

"At the Native Council center," she told him, fighting back the tremble in her voice.

"Stay there," Schiff told her. "I'll put through a quick call and have someone sent over to get you."

"Thank you."

"Listen, by the way," Schiff said, "is there a fax machine there by any chance?"

"Yes," Michelle responded, glancing at the unit on the desk beside the phone. "Why?"

"We've run off a series of altered composites based on some photos of the man we think is fronting for the Mertardans." Schiff went on to quickly explain about the aborted stakeout in Cinnaton, where the man in the blue sweats had slain Stasha Darvin.

"And you want to fax me the composites?" Michelle guessed.

"Couldn't hurt. Why don't you give me the number and I'll shoot 'em right up to you."

"Okay, fine."

Michelle read the receiving number off the fax machine, then briefed Schiff some more on her meetings in Tolnera as she waited for the composites to be printed out. There was a brief delay, then the fax engaged and a sheet of paper began to inch its way out of the machine. Slowly the image of a man's face took shape before Michelle's eyes, and she drew in her breath with horror as she recognized the same man who'd been talking with Anpard back at the cocktail lounge before his murder.

"Oh, my God!"

"What is it?"

"I know him," she whispered hoarsely. "I know who he is."

18

Agent Schiff had issued remote pagers to both Bolan and Grimaldi prior to their leaving for Tolnera, and as the two men were riding the shuttle to the work camp, both devices went off simultaneously. The pagers were equipped with digital readouts, and both men's messages were the same—CALL SCHIFF NOW. TOP PRIORITY.

"Sounds important," Grimaldi said as he scanned the readout. "Maybe we finally had a break fall our way."

"Let's get to a phone and find out," Bolan said.

The shuttle stopped at a small depot next to The Yukon Rush at the end of Main Street. Seven passengers got off with Bolan and Grimaldi while another six men boarded for the return trip to the operations center.

The inside of the depot was clean and heated, and an armed guard was stationed in the far corner to make sure it stayed that way. Along one wall was a bank of five pay phones. All of them were in use, and there were four more men waiting in line to use them.

"Damn," Grimaldi muttered.

"We can't wait," Bolan said. Producing his Justice Department credentials, he moved toward the phones, telling the other men, "Sorry, but this is an emergency. I need to use a phone."

"Emergency, my ass!" one of the workers snarled. He was a big man, six-four and more than two hundred pounds of bad attitude. His breath smelled of one too many rounds at the bar next door.

"Easy, Al," one of the other men cautioned.

"Look, we don't want any trouble here," the Executioner warned.

"No?" As Al took a threatening step toward Bolan, his friend grabbed at his arm. Al jerked himself free and swatted the Executioner's ID out of his hand. "You don't want any trouble, then get the fuck in line like everybody else!"

When the man reached out to grab Bolan, the warrior turned on him with a blinding set of karate jabs. Al never knew what hit him. He doubled over and fell to the floor with a pained groan. Meanwhile, Grimaldi whipped out his Government Model Colt and flashed his ID as well, making sure the guard could get a good look at it.

"Look, we've got enough problems already," he told the group. "Everybody just calm down and take it easy. We'll be out of here in no time."

There were murmurs of discontent, but no one else was about to try to stand up to Bolan and Grimaldi.

One of the men on the phone ended his call and handed over the receiver.

While a couple of the workers helped Al to his feet, Bolan quickly put a call through to Schiff in Fairbanks. His face darkened as the agent relayed the news about Ehki Daifreize being the terrorists' mole. As soon as he was told that Michelle had seen Daifreize with Anpard shortly before his murder, Bolan said, "Where is she?"

Schiff told him.

"Thanks, Ralph. I owe you one."

"What's up?" Grimaldi asked as Bolan hung up the receiver.

The warrior looked past Grimaldi at the security guard. "The Native Council walk-in center...where is it?"

The guard gave directions, concluding, "Only take you a couple minutes to get there if you hurry."

"Let's go," Bolan said to his friend, heading out the door.

Al cursed and tried to lunge at the Executioner but was restrained by the others. The guard moved in to maintain order as Bolan and Grimaldi stepped back into the night. Rather than holster his Colt, the pilot slipped it into the pocket of his parka for easier access. Bolan did the same with his Beretta.

"Okay, let's have it," Grimaldi demanded.

As Bolan led the way down Main Street, he quickly filled Grimaldi in on the latest developments. Grimaldi whistled low and shook his head.

"Well," he reasoned, "if this Daifreize is our man and he's here in Tolerna, then the odds are that the Mertardans are, too."

"That's right."

Bolan kept a wary eye on the shadowy doorways and side alleys as they hurried toward the walk-in center. He didn't expect to run into the terrorists, but there was a chance Daifreize was out on the prowl. Bolan was determined that if their paths crossed, he'd be ready.

The two men received their share of stares from late-night travelers, but there were no further confrontations. As the guard had told them, it took less than two minutes for them to reach the center. They walked in, interrupting a game of table tennis in the recreation room.

"We're looking for Michelle Raineswell," Bolan announced.

"Just missed her."

"Where'd she go?"

"Beats me. She rushed out like a bat out of hell. Why don't you check upstairs? That's where she was last."

Bolan thanked the men and bounded up the steps, with Grimaldi close behind. They found the secretary back at her desk, a worried look on her face. Bolan showed his ID and said, "We were supposed to meet Michelle Raineswell here. Where'd she go?"

"I don't know." The secretary was clearly flustered. "What's going on? She seemed perfectly fine when I left so she could make a phone call. When I got back, she looked like she'd seen a ghost. I asked what was wrong but she wouldn't tell me.''

"What did she do just before she left?'' Bolan asked the woman.

"Well, she was holding this,'' the woman said, picking up the fax composite of Daifreize and showing it to the men. "He's the head of the workers' union here.''

It took Bolan only a quick glance to see that Daifreize was indeed the same man who'd killed Stasha Darvin and Prince Widdar Charn.

"What else was she doing?''

The secretary thought it over, then pointed across the room. "She was standing over there by that window, just staring out. I kept asking her what was wrong, but it's like she didn't hear me. Then she just turned and grabbed the phone. She tried to call someone but the line was busy, I guess, so she threw down the phone and left. She was in such a hurry she dropped the fax, but by the time I realized it, she was already down the steps and out the door.''

As Bolan headed for the far window, Grimaldi asked the woman, "How long ago was this?''

"I don't know. Five, maybe ten minutes.''

Bolan peered out the window. There wasn't much of a view. He could see a broad field of freshly fallen snow, a small knoll, and, barely visible behind the hill, another bungalow with a truck parked next to it.

"That building out past the knoll,'' Bolan said. "What is it?''

"The union hall. It's mostly used for storage, but they have meetings there every few weeks."

"Is that the same union Ehki Daifreize is the head of?" Bolan asked.

"Yes."

Bolan whirled from the window and strode quickly toward the door. He didn't have to tell Grimaldi what he was thinking. The pilot had pieced it together, too. They left the secretary sitting dumbfounded at her desk and bounded down the stairs. By the time they were through the door, they had their guns out.

THE MOMENT she'd seen the truck parked next to the union hall, Michelle had felt certain that it had something to do with Daifreize and the terrorists. Her first inclination had been to wait for whomever Schiff had dispatched to the walk-in center and tell them about her discovery. But she'd decided against it, for two reasons. First, she was afraid that if she waited, the truck might take off, disappearing around the knoll and heading off on its mission. Secondly, since learning that someone as reputable as Ehki Daifreize had turned out to be the foremost traitor in their midst, Michelle had been filled with paranoia. Whom could she trust? What if the people Schiff notified turned out to be secret accomplices of Daifreize's? They could whisk her away and dispose of her before she could spread the alarm. She couldn't take that chance.

She'd tried to call Schiff back, but the line was busy. By then, her apprehensions had gotten the better of her. She was sure that any second the enemy would be coming through the door, pretending to be on the side of the law but secretly intent to be rid of her. She had to leave before they showed up.

And so she had run out of the walk-in center without explanation.

It had been her intention to flee as far from the union hall as possible, and yet as soon as she hit the cold open space of the field behind the center, she knew that she couldn't run away. To do so would be to betray her people just as surely as Daifreize had. Sure, a rupture in the pipeline would spell economic catastrophe for everyone in the States, but the loss to Native Alaskans would be far greater. The ruined landscape, the loss of jobs, the disruption of the ecosystem upon which the more remote tribes subsisted—her people had too much to lose if the Mertardans succeeded with their deadly plan.

No, she had to do something, and with no time to reflect on her options, she went with her instincts.

Stealing across the wintry waste, she took a roundabout course that kept the knoll between her and the union hall. As cold as it was, the snow beneath her feet was dry, making little noise as she made her way. She had no plan, no idea what she thought she might be able to do to stop the Mertardans if it was indeed their truck that was being loaded. Something. She would think of something. She had to.

Once she reached the knoll, she cautiously moved to her left until the truck and the union hall came back into view. She could see that the back tailgate of the truck was down, and several men were hauling a huge, oblong crate out of the hall and into the back of the truck. Explosives, she thought to herself. They were loading explosives.

It was going down tonight. That had to be the only possible explanation.

She moved closer, trying to get a better look. It crossed her mind that she should somehow create a disturbance, something disruptive enough that it would deter the terrorists from leaving in the truck, while at the same time drawing attention to the isolated bungalow. With any luck the legitimate authorities would respond, and hopefully they'd be armed enough to stop the Mertardans then and there.

Michelle rose from a crouch, determined to get even closer to the bungalow. However, as she stood she was startled by the sudden thrust of a gun barrel into the side of her face. She instantly knew she wasn't going anywhere.

"Well, well," Andres Gottseed drawled as he grabbed Michelle by the collar of her parka and spun her around. "Look what we have here."

EHKI DAIFREIZE SUPERVISED the transfer of the last coffin-size box from the union storage room to the back of the truck. The box, like the other two already loaded, was marked with decals and stencils as containing the specialized X-ray equipment for inspecting pipeline welds, but of course, the actual cargo was of a much different nature.

To the untrained a mere three cratefuls of assorted explosives might have seemed like a meager amount for the job at hand. When he'd first received the Mertardans' "shopping list" three months earlier, even Daifreize had been concerned that the terrorists were underestimating their task. However, he'd been assured that the bombers had carefully studied all the specs on the pipeline and felt that this amount would be more than adequate. Sure, amateurs might have needed ten times as big an arsenal, but, as evidenced by the devastation wreaked by the Mertardans' methodical bombing raids in the Persian Gulf, Daifreize knew he was dealing with professionals.

Loading completed, the Mertardans went back inside to arm themselves with 9 mm submachine guns and gather up a fourth crate filled with food rations and battery-operated field lamps and heating units. Daifreize stayed outside, smoking a cigarette and eyeing the overhead moon, which had yet to be swallowed by the advancing storm front. With any luck he figured they could have half the explosives rigged in place along the pipeline by the time they lost the moon's light, and the rest before the flurries resumed.

The truck's engine was already running, spewing a steady cloud of white exhaust from its tail pipe. As the Mertardans emerged from the bungalow with the fourth crate, Daifreize turned to flick his cigarette into the snow and was startled to see Gottseed approaching with his prisoner. The Mertardans were equally taken aback.

"Why, Ms. Raineswell," Daifreize called once he regained his composure and recognized the woman. "What brings you to this neck of the woods?"

"You aren't going to get away with this," Michelle snapped.

Daifreize smiled. "There were times I thought that, too. But not anymore. We're too close now."

"What should I do with her?" Gottseed asked.

Daifreize shrugged. "Take her inside and get rid of her." Addressing the Mertardans in Arabic, he went on, "Let's go! It's time!"

The terrorists warily began filing into the back of the truck. Gottseed seized Michelle by the arm and jerked her toward the side doorway, telling her, "Say your prayers, sweetheart."

Gottseed's head suddenly snapped sharply to one side from the impact of a .45-caliber slug. His hand fell away from Michelle's arm and he slumped against the doorjamb, eyes vacant of life, blood and ravaged tissue already beginning to spill through the gouge in his skull.

From atop the snowy knoll forty yards away, Grimaldi shifted his aim and rattled lead at the Mertardans still standing outside the truck. Two of them screamed in pain as several others scrambled for cover.

Bolan had already advanced and circled around to the back side of the bungalow. He had a clear drop on a pair of Mertardans standing off to one side of the truck. With his Beretta set on full-auto, he killed one and wounded another before being driven to cover by return fire.

Ignored during the initial commotion, Michelle bent over and snatched up Gottseed's fallen pistol. She had limited experience with firearms, but at such close range she couldn't miss gunning down the nearest Mertardan before he could raise his weapon at her.

"Get inside!" Bolan shouted to her.

Michelle followed his advice, retreating just inside the doorway. But rather than cowering and leaving things to Bolan and Grimaldi, she continued to lend a hand, keeping several of the terrorists pinned inside the truck with periodic blasts of gunfire.

Daifreize, meanwhile, spotted Grimaldi on the knoll and took a few shots at him with his Browning, then rushed forward to the truck's cab and clambered in. Releasing the parking brake, he shifted gears and rammed his foot down on the accelerator. The vehicle lunged forward, swerving as the studded tires clawed for traction on the icy roadway. The lone surviving Mertardan in back of the vehicle fired his submachine gun over the tailgate, but with the truck fishtailing his accuracy was limited.

Bolan broke away from the building, taking long zigzag strides through the snow. Bullets thumped around him but he forged on, fighting to keep his balance on the slick ground. Once he'd reached a point where the men in back couldn't see him, he veered his course and approached the truck from the passenger's side, doing his best to stay in Daifreize's blind spot. As he closed in, Grimaldi and Michelle were forced to hold their fire.

The truck picked up speed as Daifreize headed away from the work camp. Up ahead was a more traveled road, and Bolan knew that once Daifreize reached it, the truck would have better traction. He'd never be able to keep up. With a final burst of speed the Executioner moved alongside the truck, reaching his hand out until his fingers closed on the passenger's door handle. He pulled himself up, swinging his feet onto the two-runged steps below the door.

Daifreize had apparently felt Bolan board, because seconds later the passenger's window shattered from blasts from the Saudi's Browning. The warrior ducked as the shards showered around him.

As he was contemplating his next move, Bolan detected movement out of the corner of his eye. He glanced around and saw the Mertardan gunman leaning around the back end of the truck and bringing his submachine gun into firing position. Bolan whipped his Beretta around and rattled off a few rounds, one of which clipped the terrorist's shoulder. His subgun sputtered a stream of errant shots into the snow as he lost his grip on the truck and somersaulted backward over the tailgate, snapping his neck the moment he hit the ground.

That left only Daifreize and his deadly cargo to contend with.

The truck reached the service road and Daifreize immediately jerked the steering wheel sharply to one side, trying to shake Bolan off. The Executioner held on, though, shifting his weight until he had a better footing. Another shot rang inside the cab and a 9 mm slug muscled its way through the door, just missing Bolan.

As the truck straightened its course and began to pick up even more speed, the warrior tensed a moment, then swung upright, making himself an easy target as he framed himself in the passenger's window. Daifreize took his eyes off the road and raised his Browning for another shot. Bolan beat him to the trigger, drilling the Saudi with a 3-shot burst that cored his head.

Jerked to his left by the force of the kill shots, Daifreize's foot slipped off the accelerator and his hands fell from the steering wheel. The truck almost immediately began to swerve. Even though it was slowing down, Bolan was afraid there was still enough momentum for the vehicle to go out of control and leave the road. Given the amount of explosives in back, he didn't want to think of the consequences if the truck was to flip or slam into any of the concrete railings that flanked the road.

Rather than trying to save himself by jumping clear, however, Bolan leaned in through the shattered window, reaching over Daifreize's corpse. He was just barely able to get his hands on the steering wheel. By now the truck had veered across the median. The warrior fought the wheel, easing it to his right as steadily as possible.

The truck strayed across the oncoming lane onto the snow-covered gravel of the road's shoulder. The concrete railing was only four feet away.

Three... two...

The truck leveled its course just as its side panels grazed against the concrete. Bolan felt the cab vibrate and feared that even that little nudging would be enough to set off the explosion. He braced himself for the worst.

The truck slowed to a dead stop.

The Executioner yanked the keys from the ignition. He was sprawled across the front seat, propped against the man who'd drawn him into this prolonged and harrowing assignment. As he sat up, stained with his enemy's blood, Bolan exhaled with relief.

Through the front windshield, he stared out at the open road before him. Less than twenty yards away, six caribou roamed freely across the icy pavement, ignoring the truck, oblivious to any danger. In the distance the pipeline stood on its reinforced struts like a dark band across the horizon. It was still in one piece, and now, the odds were it would stay that way.

Bolan plugs a deadly hole in a Far East heroin pipeline

DON PENDLETON's

MACK BOLAN®

LETHAL IMPACT

A desperate cry for help sends Mack Bolan to the Far East to plug an expanding heroin pipeline run by the Chinese Mafia. Bolan tracks his elusive targets from the Australian outback up through Asia's underground—one man against an enemy as vast as the land itself.

Peril stalks the Executioner at every turn as he walks a fine line in this hostile killing ground, where one false step could be lethal.

CODE ZERO—the last rule of war in the fight against drugs, where losing means dying. Catch all the action in the next episode of...

CODE ZERO

D. A. HODGMAN

In Book 3: OPERATION BARBARY COAST, DEA agents Harry Wolfe and Carmelita Morales face off against the deadliest killers the other side of the drug war could put in the field.

Available in November at your favorite retail outlet.

In the 21st century, a new breed of cop
brings home the law in the latest
installment of the future law-enforcement
miniseries...

CADE

MIKE LINAKER

In the 21st-century nightmare, marshals like Thomas
Jefferson Cade carry a badge, a gun and a burning
sense of justice.

In Book 3: FIRESTREAK, Cade and his cyborg partner,
Janek, follow the bloody trail of a renegade drug
dealer to the electronic wonderland of Los Angeles and
enter the killzone...guns loaded, targets in sight.

Available in January at your favorite retail outlet.

Dan Samson finds himself a deciding factor in the Civil War in the third thrilling episode of the action miniseries...

TIMERAIDER

John Barnes

Dan Samson, a hero for all time, is thrown into the past to fight on the battlefields of history.

In Book 3: UNION FIRES, the scene has switched to the Civil War, and Vietnam veteran Dan Samson works to free a leading member of the biggest resistance group in the South.

Available in December at your favorite retail outlet.